Curse Unwound

DEEPAK BHOOTRA

INDIA • SINGAPORE • MALAYSIA

ISBN
Paperback 979-8-89446-381-0
Hardcase 979-8-89544-881-6

Dedication

This book is a heartfelt tribute to my mother, Neelam, whose unwavering resilience has been my guiding light since birth. It is also a homage to the enchanting city of Jodhpur, my birthplace and the nurturing ground of my formative years.

Jodhpur, often called the 'Blue City' of Rajasthan, India, is a mesmerising fusion of beauty, history, and culture. It holds a special place in my heart as the backdrop of my formative years when I was enveloped by the warmth and vibrancy of its people and surroundings. It's where I imbibed a deep reverence for heritage, tradition, and diversity and where my love for storytelling took root.

As you embark on this literary journey, I hope you will be transported to the enchanting world of Jodhpur and get a taste of its captivating charm and profound heritage. I am deeply grateful for your presence in this narrative, and I look forward to sharing this journey with you.

Table of Contents

Chapter 1:

The Decaying Elderly Man

"To save the family, abandon a man. To save the village, abandon a family; to save the country, abandon a village; to save the soul, abandon the earth."

"The Mahabharata, Volume 2, Book of the Assembly Hall," p. 131.

Translated and edited by J.A.B. van Buitenen.

The room sat at the intersection of two worlds: minimalistic yet opulent. The pristine white walls stood tall like guardians, their simplicity contrasting with the space's opulence. The atmosphere was tense, as if afraid to disrupt the delicate equilibrium.

In the middle of the room, an elderly man lay alone on a simple bed. An oxygen mask partially covered his face, and the rhythmic beeping of the life-support machine broke the silence, marking the passage of time like a solemn metronome.

His skin clung to his bones, translucent and delicate, bearing witness to the years that had passed. His once lively eyes now held shadows, revealing the accumulation of joys and sorrows etched into their depths. Despite his ageing, his mind remained sharp, skilfully navigating through the maze of memories that tugged at his consciousness.

A nurse quietly approached to care for him tenderly, contradicting his inner turmoil. She tended to his delicate form, which held a multitude of life experiences. This rich mosaic chronicled his journey through happiness and sorrow, love and loss, creating patterns that sharply contrasted with the clinical environment.

Then, there was the box, a significant relic. Unassuming, yet its weight transcended its physical form. His eyes brightened as he traced the letters of his name etched on its lid: "Avinash Bhati." Pride surged within him, dwarfing the frailty of his body. This box held more than mere souvenirs; it cradled legacies— stories waiting to be told.

Within these weathered confines, treasures were to be found. Faded news clippings chronicling triumphs, a tarnished medal whispering of courage, and other emblems of a fully-lived life. Each artefact tells a story: the heady scent of victory, the bittersweet taste of sacrifice. They bridge time, connecting Avinash to vivid moments spanning years.

He felt the worn edges of an old newspaper clipping, its print faded but still meaningful. An award for bravery, tarnished with green, now stood for endurance. These items weren't just things but links to his history, pulsing with significance.

As he touched each item, the room grew still. A rush of memories returned: bright flowers in the sunlight, children playing, and the comfort of his wife's hug. Feelings of regret and yearning turned into hope, softening the harshness of the walls around him. In his sorrow, Avinash found comfort, a refuge within the room. His emotional journey, from regret to hope, is one that many can empathise with.

The machines' beeping faded away, replaced by echoes of the past. He allowed himself to be swept up in it, immersed in memories that connected him to a vividly lived past filled with wonder. The sterile room transformed into a space infused with Avinash's spirit, a backdrop for his colourful recollections. In this tranquillity, he celebrated the moments of a fulfilling life, mindful that his legacy would endure as a timeless melody even as his strength diminished.

The nurse approached his side, her face mirroring the sadness etched on Avinash. However, when she tried to help, he waved her away, not tearing his eyes from the captivating contents of the box. This was his sacred journey into memory. Yet, he knew someone else wanted to join him, bridging the chasm of time to be acknowledged.

The room was filled with silence, occasionally broken by the creak of wood underfoot or the faint chirps of birds outside. A young man sat nervously on a chair near Avinash's bed, fidgeting. His gaze darted across the meticulously arranged items, seeking to break the silence. While he longed to glimpse his father's world, he also respected his need for reflection. Thus, he stayed put, waiting for a sign.

Despite facing age and health challenges, Avinash Bhati's presence evoked awe and admiration in his son, Vaibhav Bhati. As their eyes met, a silent communication passed between them, revealing the depth of their bond. Through a simple yet powerful gesture, the older man called Vaibhav closer, conveying a wealth of wisdom and love.

Walking towards his father, Vaibhav moved with hesitation and curiosity. As he got closer, he noticed a spark of emotion in Avinash's stoic face. For a moment, the familiar lines of pain on the elderly face softened to an expression of warm anticipation. A deep connection and enduring affection united father and son in that meaningful moment.

Avinash gently laughed with pride in his voice as he lightly pressed against the surface of an aged photograph.

"Look at this moment where I posed next to Madiba following his prison release in 1992. I was rather dapper, wasn't I?"

Clutching the photo delicately, he reminisced about that time with a mix of weariness and fondness. Although fatigue showed on his face, a gentle smile lit it up as he gently placed his trembling hand over his heart.

Vaibhav watched intently as his father tenderly handled the photograph. Their eyes were collectively drawn to the pair memorialised within it. He had grown up immersed in tales of his father's storied encounter with the legendary Nelson Mandela, the first president of South Africa after the country emerged out of Apartheid. The image stirred a wave of potent emotions.

The older man let out a gentle sigh as his features relaxed. In a whisper filled with emotion, he confided, "Meeting him was a defining moment in my journey. It's a memory I'll cherish forever." Though his voice hinted at fatigue, a tenacity underlying it ignited inspiration in Vaibhav. Avinash began to speak, but a sudden coughing fit left him flustered and agitated. The box slid off the bed to the ground with a crash. Its contents scattered across the floor, disrupting Avinash's moment of discomfort. Amidst the scattered items, he caught sight of a photograph that had escaped the box. In the photo, a younger Avinash and his bride, Jyoti, were dressed in Rajput bridal attire, exuding joy and celebration. Jyoti looked elegant in her vibrant dress, accentuated with gold threading and reflective mirrors, while Avinash appeared dignified in his ornate turban and splendid ceremonial wear.

The colourful past came rushing back into Avinash's consciousness. His eyes fluttered as he remembered the vivid sensation of flower petals being cast down in celebration, echoing the rhythmic pulse of drums set against a backdrop of the night sky, punctuated with stars.

The room became a time capsule haunted by the relics of his glorious exploits, showcasing his valorous

youth during royal hunts. However, these remnants didn't bring comfort; instead, they stirred up a storm of unrest, reminding him of past joy conflicting with present hardships.

The elderly gentleman carefully took out a worn envelope covered in exotic stamps from the box. It was a souvenir from many decades ago, containing a letter he had written to his beloved wife, Jyoti, when circumstances arising from a sudden business trip forced them apart shortly after their wedding. Avinash handed the envelope to his son, Vaibhav, and encouraged him to read it aloud. His voice expressed excitement and longing as he tried reliving cherished memories through his son's narration.

Vaibhav hesitated, torn between his curiosity and respect for a private message meant for his mother. Eventually, he chose to honour his father's request. Carefully unfolding the fragile pages, he read his father's words out loud.

Dear Jyoti,

The ink flows like the river that separates us – fast and unending, carrying the weight of longing. My heart remains tied to you in this distant city, surrounded by unfamiliar faces and the babel of business.

The nights feel endless without your laughter and warmth. The hotel room is impersonal and empty without you. I picture your smile – the way it crinkles at the corners, the silent language it shares with your eyes. I yearn to touch those lines with my fingertips.

My days blend meetings, negotiations, and the constant pursuit of success. But success feels empty without you. I find myself checking the time difference, wondering if you're drinking your morning tea or gazing at the same moon that illuminates me.

Remember our walks by the river? The way we held hands, our fingers entwined like promises. Each step was a promise to face challenges together, find joy every day, and build a life filled with love. As I walk these unfamiliar streets, I long for your hand in mine.

Jyoti, my love, I carry you with me. Your laughter dances in the margins of my reports, and your scent lingers on my shirt collar. I close my eyes, and there you are, vibrant and irreplaceable.

I yearn to talk to you, to hear about the garden and the roses you care for. When night falls, picture me with you. Share our secrets with the moon, and know that I'm listening. Our love is a guide that leads me home.

Until then, my Jyoti, hold our memories close. They are the compass that brings me back to you.

Yours forever, Avinash.

Vaibhav found himself unable to speak, his eyes glistening with emotion. As he tried to offer comforting words, his father sharply interrupted with a stern tone.

"Our heritage is that of warriors, expected to die in battle or fade with honourable scars. This illness, a thief stealing from me before my time, demands sacrifices beyond my ability," he conveyed, his vibrant spirit fading.

The atmosphere grew heavy with profound revelation as he grasped Vaibhav's hand with the desperation of a drowning man reaching for a lifeline. His plea cut through the solemn atmosphere of the room. "I beg you to free our family from this curse that casts a shadow over our days." His words were a mix of urgency and solemnity, profoundly resonating with Vaibhav.

The nurse recognised signs of distress and decisively moved to assist. Vaibhav attentively watched as she silently adjusted the morphine drip's valve, with the device steadily administering pain relief to his father. The room's soft light relieved the creases of concern on her forehead, revealing her intense commitment to patient care. Vaibhav remained quietly impressed by her precise and careful actions, finding comfort in her steadfast dedication.

His father exhaled deeply and settled back into the hospital bed, his body relaxing after the recent stressful ordeal. Vaibhav noticed a gentle shift in his father's facial expression; a look of peaceful calm slowly replaced the marks of pain and anxiety. The creases in his father's forehead softened, and a quiet smile appeared.

Vaibhav was moved by the powerful impact of the medication, which provided his father with a break from the harsh reality of his illness. He imagined a comforting warmth easing all his father's pain and suffering. He silently expressed gratitude for the nurse's compassionate care and the medicine's effective relief. Although he knew this relief was only temporary, it was crucial, as his father found comfort from pain in those moments. As he watched his father drift into a peaceful sleep, Vaibhav felt deeply thankful for this short moment of tranquillity amidst their ongoing challenges.

Seated diligently by his father's side, Vaibhav embraced the role of a watchful protector with a heart heavy with concern and care. For the past several months, he had been a silent witness to the relentless and heart-wrenching deterioration of his father's once robust health. The unyielding grip of illness had chipped away at his father's indomitable spirit, transforming him into a mere shadow of his former self. During the rare moments of respite brought by medication-induced rest, the deep lines etched by suffering on his father's visage softened, briefly revealing fleeting glimpses of the vibrant and resilient man he had been before the onset of illness.

In the soft glow that filled the room, Vaibhav's gaze came to rest upon the intricately designed wooden box, its aged surface weathered by the inevitable passage of time. He sifted through the contents that had spilt from within with utmost care and reverence.

Among them were weathered letters, each containing a story of its own; faded photographs capturing moments frozen in time; and an old pocket watch, its well-worn case holding the quiet mystery of countless bygone days. He placed the box on a nearby table and allowed it to bask in the ethereal light pouring through the expansive window, permeating the room with a profound sense of tranquillity.

Under the soft, silvery glow of the moonlight, Vaibhav stood in deep contemplation near the towering windows of his family's ancestral home. His eyes fixated on the majestic outline of Houghton Ridge, looming against the backdrop of the sparkling Johannesburg night sky. Amid this serene moment, a profound realisation began to take shape in his mind – one that could relieve a long-held secret burdening his father and possibly dispel the lingering sorrow that had plagued their family for countless generations. It was a revelation that carried with it the weight of forever altering the course of their lives.

With determination etched into his features, Vaibhav considered reaching out to Candice Kruger. With a resolve as unyielding as the Houghton Ridge against the night sky, Vaibhav swiftly left the room, driven by the urgency of his newfound purpose.

He was acutely aware of the weightiness of seeking Candice's assistance, realising that it might necessitate her temporary departure from the demanding legal sphere. Despite the demanding responsibilities entailed in overseeing a vast business empire, he steeled himself for his father's sake, hoping to enlist Candice's astute legal mind and unwavering resolve.

As his father's health continued to decline, the relentless march of time hung heavily over him, heightening the urgency of every precious moment amidst their challenging circumstances. The mounting pressure felt akin to an unseen adversary, with his father's fate hanging in the balance. Yet, against the backdrop of the glittering urban nightscape, Vaibhav's unwavering focus on achieving justice remained unshakeable, propelled by an unyielding resolve to bring solace to his father and their entire family before time inevitably slipped away.

Chapter 2:

By His Deathbed

"He who has felt the deepest grief is best able to experience supreme happiness. Live, then, and be happy, beloved children of my heart, and never forget that until the day God shall deign to reveal the future to man, all human wisdom is summed up in these two words – wait and hope."

– Alexandre Dumas, The Count of Monte Cristo

With her heart thumping against her ribcage, Candice Kruger walked resolutely away from the entrance of the law firm she once called home. Each heartbeat resonated with her intentional, carefully considered decision to pursue a new path away from her secure position in corporate law. Her finely made wool coat, designed to flatter her slim frame, did little to shield her from the harsh winter of Johannesburg. The piercing cold cut through her attire, chilling her to the bone, mainly as her neck remained exposed under her neat ponytail. Pulling her coat's lapels closer, she steeled herself against the frigid air, ready to face whatever obstacles awaited her.

Candice had decided to sell her share of the prestigious law firm she once co-managed and chose to take some time to reconsider and contemplate her future goals. As she stood on the bustling street, bathed in the soft light of dusk, she felt a wave of nostalgia as she gazed at the building where she had dedicated over a decade of her professional life. The structure, with its imposing facade and large windows, was filled with emotions and memories – it was where she grew from a determined associate to a respected partner. This was also where she made significant personal sacrifices while relentlessly pursuing success. She amassed considerable wealth within those walls, representing influential corporations across Africa. Her memories were a mix of tales of her achievements and sacrifices.

Candice felt a mix of emotions as she stood before the tall building. Despite her success in corporate law, she felt increasingly dissatisfied. She knew that change was necessary for her to focus on important causes and make a real impact. With both uncertainty and determination, she took a deep breath and stepped into an unpredictable but exciting future. Even though leaving her secure past was scary, she was ready to embrace the unknown and work towards significant progress. She saw the path ahead as an exciting journey she was eager to embark on with complete determination.

As Candice walked towards the luxurious sedan, her heels clicking against the pavement, she felt the day's strain begin to lift. She was meeting Vaibhav Bhati, a college peer and long-time client, for a sudden meeting. Although she found his enigmatic manner perplexing, their long-term connection reassured her. Bhati's businesses had significantly expanded over the years, benefiting her as well. She anticipated receiving ad hoc assignments from them during her transition and transformation period. She felt empowered and prepared to address forthcoming challenges and make a significant impact on society through her future endeavors.

As she arrived at the luxurious vehicle, the chauffeur opened the back passenger door for her. Inside, she found Vaibhav Bhati exuding calm composure. Candice greeted him with a nod and removed her coat, revealing her exquisitely crafted designer suit.

"Vaibhav," she began in a mock stern tone, "you've been eager all week to arrange this meeting to discuss assisting your father with a personal issue. I'm trying to grasp what's at stake here. How is your dad managing his sickness? It's been four or five years since I last saw him. Why is it important that we talk now? Is he okay? What should I be aware of?" Her furrowed brow showed she was expecting an answer.

Vaibhav, showing a hint of resignation, clasped his hands before responding. "Yes, you're always one for getting straight to the point," he remarked before praising Candice's achievements. He then shifted the conversation towards the critical issue, his eyes darting with concern.

"You've played a key role in our growth plans. My father, Avinash, respects you a lot. His health has significantly deteriorated, and I'm afraid he's nearing the end. Please approach this meeting with an open mind and patience," he asked with a heavy heart, hesitantly releasing his clasped hands. With a weighty sigh, he paused and then continued.

"Father is deteriorating rapidly and needs immediate help with a personal matter that requires someone as straightforward and practical as you," he explained. Noticing the puzzled expression on Candice's face, he elaborated.

"You last saw my father at my wedding five years ago when he was vibrant and strong. He's closely followed your legal support for our expansion in Southern Africa. Learning of your decision to leave the corporate world surprised him, yet he was glad about your availability for occasional consulting, given your familiarity with our family business. I need your expertise urgently to handle a sensitive personal affair."

Candice appeared intrigued as Vaibhav spoke. She kept her composure, crossing her arms defensively and leaning back as she probed Vaibhav for more details.

"Yes, I can assist in planning his estate in the event of his passing, but I know your father can access that kind of support from in-house lawyers. Why do they want my services? There's more to this, isn't there?"

Vaibhav weakly smiled and tried to explain further. "My family has royal lineage from Rajasthan in India..."

Before he could continue, Candice politely interrupted him, urging him to get to the point. She eagerly awaited a thorough response to a simple question about the upcoming meeting. The driver accelerated as if in response to Candice's impatient inquiries. With a touch of scepticism, Candice kept her lips sealed but gave Vaibhav her full attention as he elaborated.

As the car smoothly navigated through the bustling city streets towards the opulent residences of Houghton Ridge in Johannesburg, Candice and Vaibhav engaged in a heartfelt discussion about his father's declining health. The memory of Avinash's imposing presence at Vaibhav's grand wedding reception five years earlier lingered vividly in Candice's thoughts.

What a fantastic wedding it was! The entire event was filled with excitement. Candice wore a stunning gown inspired by the vibrant colours of India. She was captivated by the unfolding rituals—the sacred fire, the exchange of garlands, and the whispered vows. Vaibhav's parents beamed with pride. The wedding banquet was a sensory delight—fragrant Indian delicacies and intricate desserts. She struggled with the spices in the dishes but thoroughly enjoyed herself. She smiled as she remembered the event and glanced out of the window. They were approaching

Houghton. A rich tapestry of heritage and luxury unfolded before their eyes, with majestic mansions serving as a testament to generations of prosperity amassed from the abundant gold and minerals in South Africa's fertile soil. The car elegantly traversed the grand streets, passing meticulously manicured lawns and splendid homes that whispered stories of enduring wealth.

The car smoothly passed through the imposing iron gates and halted on a gravel driveway in front of an impressive, stately mansion. The mansion loomed ominously against a backdrop of dense woodlands. When Candice stepped out of the vehicle, a profound silence enveloped her. They proceeded through the main entrance and along an ornate hallway. A woman gracefully emerged from a side door, her form accentuated by the glowing lights. Adorned in a striking magenta and gold outfit, she approached with an air of refinement. She reached for Candice's hands immediately, offering a warm welcome. It was Vaibhav's mother, Jyoti.

Grasping Candice's hands, Jyoti spoke with a hint of nostalgia in a melodic tone. "Welcome to our home, my dear. It's a pleasure to have met you after such a long time. I've been eagerly looking forward to this moment. It feels like ages since we last crossed paths at Vaibhav's wedding."

Despite the years since they last saw each other, Candice found immediate comfort in Jyoti's velvety voice. Jyoti's genuine and warm welcome was reciprocated with Candice's smile as they ended their embrace.

As they approached a large hall at the end of the hallway, Candice was filled with wonder, taking in the generous space. Although familiar with the estate, this was her first time entering its living quarters as she had only visited the office suite for business purposes.

Jyoti graciously offered Candice a seat in the luxurious surroundings. Soft lighting brought the velvet chairs with gold accents and intricate patterns to life, casting a spell over the space. Surrounded by such grandeur, Candice let her gaze wander over the extravagant details.

The space was adorned with exquisite wooden elements and furniture, each showcasing exceptional craftsmanship with elaborate carvings. Tapestries depicting scenes from Indian legends in vibrant, rich colours and meticulous artistry adorned the area, each weaving a captivating story through its intricate design.

Candice was captivated by the vibrant frescoes that adorned the walls. The murals depicted divine figures and epic heroes with stunning precision and colour, drawing Candice into the lore they depicted.

Feeling overwhelmed by the grandeur of her surroundings, Candice was transported to a magical realm steeped in fascination and beauty. Every aspect invited her to appreciate the splendour around her.

One tapestry, portraying an Indian goddess amidst elephants and blooming lotus flowers, demanded Candice's attention. Detailed with golden threads, the goddess's garment glistened in the room's subtle light, creating a fascinating effect. Just as Candice contemplated the exquisite artistry of the work, Jyoti interrupted her thoughts.

"I will take you to Avinash," Jyoti said, leading Candice towards a large door at the end of another corridor. Vaibhav smiled pensively at his mother but did not follow. Candice glanced over her shoulder, but he nodded in assurance and waved her on.

"Avinash does not meet many people due to his sickness, but he has been anxiously waiting to meet you," Jyoti explained. Candice tried to recall her last interaction with Avinash, but her thoughts were interrupted by Jyoti's continued small talk about the family.

Candice walked into a chamber that smelled like antiseptic, feeling nervous with every step. A nurse dressed in calming blue led her through dim hallways to a seat next to the bed, offering a gentle smile that struggled to cut through the solemn atmosphere. As she sat down, Candice's eyes fell on Avinash, unmoving amidst the noise of life-support equipment, their eerie light casting ghostly shadows. The vigour surrounding him was now reduced to murmurs among the tangled tubes and wires, a silent testament to his struggle.

The sight of Avinash, once vibrant and now diminished, painfully twisted Candice's reality. Her eyes searched his features in the low light, grief swelling as she witnessed the battle etched in every shuddering breath he took. It was a harrowing spectacle, an unjust transformation from the person he once was to the near apparition he had become. Surrounded by what seemed like orchestral murmurs of medical equipment, feelings of despair surged within her.

Avinash's weak yet determined whisper against the ventilator's steady chant broke the oppressive stillness. He lay there, a figure of frailty and quiet resistance, the undulating mask upon his face underscoring each precious breath and concealing a faint but significant smile.

His voice was rough and laboured as he said, "Candice, you shine just as you did five years back at Vaibhav's wedding." He noted your departure from the law firm to concentrate on select issues. "I'm running out of time, and I have an important tale to share, Candice, a story that's haunted my family for centuries. May I go on?"

Candice was taken aback by Avinash's weakened state and his sudden shift into a narrative that highlighted her limited understanding of the situation. She warily assented, feeling her heartbeat rise in the solemn atmosphere surrounding them. As the elderly man struggled to adjust himself in bed, the visible deterioration of his health was distressing. However, despite the difficult circumstances, Candice felt a begrudging responsibility to listen attentively.

Jyoti and Candice were drawn to each other under the soft light from the window. With a gentle touch, Jyoti guided Candice to a comfortable loveseat near the bed, where they could sit closely together, comforted by the soft upholstery. Avinash's gentle yet persistent voice filled the space as the room fell silent, captivating Candice and transporting her to ancient India. Despite his frail appearance, his presence commanded attention, holding Candice spellbound with every word. Fully engrossed in this enigmatic and captivating narrative, she prepared herself for a complex journey, staying true to her promise to follow his poignant tale with undivided attention.

Captivated by every syllable, she watched Avinash's strength wane, only to be seamlessly replaced by Jyoti, whose voice ebbed and flowed like liquid gold, weaving a tapestry of love and adventure from centuries ago as she took over the thread from an exhausted Avinash. The story's unique intricacies piqued Candice's interest, eliciting a subtle raise of her eyebrows. Yet, she remained fixed on her intent, listening with unwavering focus.

Candice slowly lowered her defences, surrendering to the allure of mystery and romance woven carefully into the narrative. With each passing moment, she felt herself succumbing to the captivating dance of imagination and fascination. The world around them seemed to fade into the background as Jyoti's storytelling conjured vivid, enchanting images in Candice's mind. It was as if she had been transported into the tale, experiencing every emotion and sensation alongside the characters. In that suspended moment, nothing existed except for the enthralling story unfolding before her.

Chapter 3:

The Smitten Prince

"I am glad it cannot happen twice, the fever of first love. For it is a fever and a burden, too, whatever the poets may say."

– Daphne du Maurier

Prince Bhanwar moved with the precision of a skilled hunter. His senses were heightened, every muscle coiled and ready for the next calculated step. The sun beat down on the dry earth, causing sweat on his forehead. He carefully scanned the patchy greenery with sharp eyes, alert for movement. When he heard a faint sound, he knew his target was nearby.

Through years of relentless training, he had honed his reflexes, allowing him to remain steady as he effortlessly drew the arrow back on his box. As the black buck appeared, bathed in sunlight, Prince Bhanwar scrutinised every detail intensely. A triumphant smile formed on his lips as he silently expressed gratitude to the goddess of the hunt for her constant favour.

Prince Bhanwar embodied the very essence of a natural-born stalker, melting into the backdrop with feral finesse, a shadow among the sparse grass. The target locked in his gaze, his body strung tight like his drawn bowstring. He exhaled one focused breath and readied for the release. However, just as he was about to release his arrow, a sudden shout shattered the tranquillity of the forest, disrupting his carefully laid plans. "Stop!"

The hunt was abruptly interrupted, allowing the majestic buck to escape. To his surprise, he spotted a Banjara tribal girl on a tree branch, her bold gaze fixed.

Dressed in black with shimmering gold details and jingling anklets, she held a small spear, ready to jump down skillfully.

Frustrated, Prince Bhanwar watched as the composed and self-assured girl faced his approaching soldiers without fear. He ordered them to stop and took control of the situation, drawing his weapon on the courageous challenger.

"Do you wish to feel this arrow pierce your heart? You foolish girl, how dare you take away from me my God-given birthright?" Prince Bhanwar's voice dripped with disbelief and outrage.

"God-given birthright!" the girl repeated in a mockingly animated tone, effectively punctuating her disdain for his words.

Bhanwar's expression contorted astonishment as he grappled to comprehend her audacious defiance.

His response faltered, caught off guard by her swift and incisive retort. However, the girl remained resolute, locking eyes with him, her unwavering determination shining through her fiery gaze as she firmly asserted her challenge.

"What else does the good Lord permit you to claim as your own? You speak of God yet show no respect for his creations. How dare you needlessly take their lives and invoke his name in doing so?" Her pointed gesture to the sky underscored her reference to God, her eyes ablaze with fiery intensity.

The prince's expression darkened at the insult and blatant disrespect in her voice. A rush of heat flooded his cheeks as he struggled to maintain his composure. Despite the humiliation of the situation, he couldn't help but be taken aback by the girl's courageous confrontation. Standing tall, her defiant posture exuded confidence; with her small pointed spear poised, she held the prince captive with a piercing gaze. His mind reeling, he mustered the strength to direct a simple question towards her.

"You talk of respect, yet here you are with a spear. What business does one have with instruments of death in a dense forest? It is a precursor of nefarious intent, is it not?"

The girl listened to Bhanwar's question and smiled with mild disdain. She puckered her lips and replied with a snide tone, "These instruments of death are not for the animals here but rather for the inhuman beasts like you who come here to hurt and maim needlessly."

The soldiers had been watching but glanced furtively, trying to figure out a response or reaction. It is evident to them that the girl was no ordinary woman. She remained fearless despite being surrounded by soldiers. The girl's insolence prompted one of the soldiers to rush up to her and grab her hair, forcing her to her knees while shouting, "Apologise to Prince Bhanwar, or I will behead you!"

The girl remained unfazed and addressed the prince with a condescending tone. "If this is the reward I get for saving one of God's creations, so be it. But if this is punishment for intervening in some vain man's attempt to prove he is mightier than an unarmed antelope, then it is nothing but murder."

As she turned towards the prince, the veil that covered and partially obscured her radiant face fell off, exposing her long, dense tresses, alabaster skin, and lips like soft, red roses.

"Be off with you, girl!" snarled Bhanwar, jabbing his finger at her. "Do not test my patience, or else…"

The young woman couldn't hold back her laughter. She looked the prince in the eyes and then turned away, her voice unwavering as she gestured upward. "We Banjaras are not easily intimidated. Your empty threats mean nothing to me. You've always had everything handed to you on a silver platter, but today, you've learned that life isn't always fair. I hope you enjoyed the lesson."

As she made her way further, the prince watched her with admiration. He was struck by her elegant and assured movements, thoroughly enchanted by her. Her dark hair flowed down her back, shimmering in the sunlight and casting intriguing shadows. With every step, it was as if she were in sync with nature, moving with a rhythmic grace through the rough terrain, resembling a dancer rather than a mere walker.

His focused gaze lingered on her, seeing beyond her surface beauty and the undeniable charisma that emanated from her. Her poised posture, confident demeanour, and purposeful strides conveyed an inherent, authoritative presence that naturally commanded attention and respect. Despite lacking noble birth, she carried herself with such regal grace that it was impossible to overlook. Her piercing gaze communicated pride without words as she glanced back at him, leaving him curious about the depths concealed beneath her seemingly straightforward exterior. She possessed a magnetic allure that set her apart significantly, especially compared to his nobility.

That night, as he sat thoughtfully next to the flickering campfire, he couldn't stop thinking about how she had looked at him. The image of the Banjara girl kept coming back to him like fireflies dancing in the dark. He felt a mysterious pull at his heart, leaving him unsettled. His sleep was troubled, filled with a longing for their paths to cross again. However, he knew he had to return to the safety of his royal residence in Mandore for the time being.

As the prince's entourage prepared for their onward journey, a group of men dressed in traditional

Banjara clothing emerged from the outskirts of the camp. Their hands were raised in respect as they approached the prince's tents. Requesting an audience with the prince, they were acknowledged with a nod. The prince, intrigued by their presence, inquired, "Pray tell, who are you, and what is the purpose of your visit?"

The leader of the group, distinguished by a bright, multi-coloured turban, stepped forward and bowed. "Your Highness, I am Chief Nagarmal," he said. "Our Banjara community lives in a nearby village by Bal Samand Lake," he added respectfully. "We are your devoted subjects and would be greatly honoured if you would agree to visit our village, enjoy our hospitality, and grace us with your presence before you proceed on your travels."

"Thank you," said Bhanwar with a broad smile. "Your kindness is appreciated."

The prince issued loud orders to his troops, instructing them to prepare for the unplanned route. He climbed onto his horse with a determined gait, joining Chief Nagarmal and the Banjara tribe on their way to their settlement, intrigued and eager about what lay ahead.

As the prince and his entourage traversed the rugged terrain, they finally reached the outskirts of the village. A small but exuberant group welcomed them, their faces reflecting deep respect and happiness. The villagers bowed as the prince and his party passed by. The prince was grateful for the warm reception, especially as he recalled the previous night's events. His mind meandered to the thought of Neelam. The image of the Banjara girl was burned into his mind and being.

In a poignant moment, he noticed a figure on the crowd's fringes– the same girl who had thwarted his triumphant hunt! She was seated calmly among the adoring villagers. His frustration surged as he clenched his fists, and disbelief filled his widened eyes, for she remained unperturbed while others fussed around in admiration.

Prince Bhanwar pointed his finger at the girl and turned to Chief Nagarmal, expressing his frustration, "Nagarmal, that vile girl ruined my hunt yesterday and disrespected me in front of my soldiers! I want her to apologise for her behaviour and disrespect!"

Neelam stood defiantly, her eyes flashing brighter than the polished gemstones in the prince's crown. Her defiance was a legacy passed down from generations of strong-willed Banjara women.

Neelam refused to apologise, and Nagarmal's heart sank. He had hoped for a swift resolution – a nod, a muttered sorry – and then they could move on. But Neelam's silence was a declaration, a refusal to bow before anyone, even a prince. Her silence spoke of pride, defiance, and perhaps a touch of recklessness.

Prince Bhanwar's gaze shifted from Nagarmal to Neelam, assessing them both.

"Let her be," he said, his voice soft but commanding. "She is beyond forgiveness. She is incapable of repenting for her disrespect to me."

Nagarmal's heart clenched. Beyond forgiveness? Repent? What had Neelam done? He stole a glance at Neelam. He sensed a storm coming as her jaw was set, her nostrils flaring. She was ready to defend her actions, consequences be damned.

Neelam's retort was swift, fuelled by anger and a sense of justice. "Repent? I will never repent for my actions! You deserve no respect, a person who kills only for sport or pleasure!"

Nagarmal's loyalty wavered, torn between duty and love. The prince's gaze remained steady on Neelam's angry face. Neelam's defiance reflected the complexities of their existence, a precarious dance on the edge of power and morality.

Chief Nagarmal was visibly distressed and sought to shield Neelam from the prince's gaze. Turning to the prince, he pleaded for forgiveness, "My Lord, she is my daughter Neelam, and I humbly apologise for her behaviour."

The prince was taken aback upon learning that Neelam was Nagarmal's daughter, but he couldn't help but feel a rush of emotions. Concealing a smile, he suggested to the chief and his men that they extend their visit to enjoy Nagarmal's hospitality fully. Nagarmal and the villagers warmly welcomed this suggestion.

As the full moon rose in the dark blue night sky, an extravagant feast occurred in a lush green field. The air was filled with traditional music and laughter as people enjoyed various delicious and aromatic dishes.

Neelam joined the festivities, singing a heartfelt song about her longing for a lost love. Her voice carried sorrow and anticipation like a gentle breeze on a balmy evening.

With grace and elegance, she began dancing as the music became tempo.

In the realm where golden dunes reside,
Suns of saffron kiss the earth's hide,
A tale of vibrant tunes takes stride,
Of dreams that glide with every birth.
Among the cacti and sage, so wide,
Two souls by a hidden oasis abide,
Her laughter, like a monsoon on a parched page's tide,
His gaze is a mirage of promises that hide.
They dance to the melodies of the wind,
His turban, a crimson swirl, her veil, a blue tide.
Their love, a storm of whispers, confides.
They reside in the shifting sands, forever pure.
They glide under the silver crescent.
Her anklets chime, his heartbeat in sync,
and they lay beside each other.
Saffron dreams with desert salt collide.

In body and soul, they become unified.

But the day came when he left to fight outside; she stayed for his return and patiently bided.

She prayed to the stars that he would survive.

and hoped their love would never subside.

She roams the barren land,

Her words coincided,

"Come back to me, my betrothed," she cries.

She searches for his traces in every stride;

She longs for his touch in every tide.

Where your scent fills the air, wide,

Where the dunes sing of your beauty,

Where the stars, for you alone, provide,

Where, with a restless heart, I reside.

Ages have passed, yet inside,

The thought of my sweetheart beside me is still with me.

a constant guide;

Your memories reside in every corner of my being.

My fingers have gone rough counting the time,

and their lines have subsided.

In some way, my fortune has been set aside,

When thunder crackles, I hide;

My tears will cease only when you grace my side,

All my emotional yearnings will be satisfied,

This desolate world, at me, it scolds.

Come back to me, my fickle betrothed,

I cried. For you, constantly, I bide.

But the night brought me a dreadful sight:

A messenger with a letter in his hand.

He told me the news shattered my life:

You had fallen in the battle, defending your land.

My heart broke into a thousand pieces,

And my soul screamed in agony.

I collapsed to the ground, clutching your name.

How could fate be so cruel and uncanny?

Where your scent filled the air, wide,

Where the dunes sang of your beauty,

Where the stars for you alone provided,

Where, with a broken heart, I reside.

Now, I sing this song of grief and pride.

and love that transcended death and strife.

I wait for the day when we will reunite.

In the realm where golden dunes reside.

Prince Bhanwar was utterly absorbed and spellbound by the captivating show before him. When Neelam began to sing, her melodious voice filled the air and touched him deeply. The resonating notes were powerful and profoundly moving, awakening a solid longing and connection within him.

Neelam's presence was enchanting. Her movements gracefully expressed the essence of the music, conveying a range of emotions with gentle precision. The interplay of light and shadow highlighted her transcendent charm, enhancing the feeling of yearning and affection in her performance.

As he watched, Prince Bhanwar was engulfed in various feelings, combining to form a striking representation of longing. The impact of Neelam's entrancing exhibition lingered with him long after it concluded, imprinting upon his memory and resisting the pull of obscurity.

Throughout the night, as he attempted to sleep, thoughts of Neelam filled his mind. He imagined sharing dances and quiet moments with her under the stars, their connection speaking volumes of unspoken emotions. In the sanctuary of his dreams, he visualised tender kisses and heartfelt conversations illuminated by the moon. Amidst his restless sleep, he envisioned a life unrestricted by obligations, brimming with passion and happiness, with Neelam as his steadfast companion, creating an enduring bond.

# Chapter 4:

A 300-Year-Old Love Story

"Love is an untamed force. When we try to control it, it destroys us. When we try to imprison it, it enslaves us. When we try to understand it, it leaves us feeling lost and confused."

– Paulo Coelho

The next day, Prince Bhanwar decided to walk by the calm and picturesque lake. This serene lakeside held within it a wealth of hidden stories whispered by the gentle, rippling waters and sheltered by the ancient, towering trees that stood guard along its shores. Carrying the weight of his noble lineage and the burden of great expectations, the prince sought solace in the tranquillity of this place. The water, mirroring his restless thoughts, also reflected the saffron hues of the sky above, promising something more.

Walking by the peaceful waterside, he was greeted by a breathtaking sight. Neelam was riding a camel in the shallow waters, illuminated by the soft, early morning sunlight. The camel sported an exquisite, ornate saddle that showcased the craftsmanship and expertise of the desert communities. Crafted from fine leather, it was beautifully adorned with vivid red, blue,

and green shades, featuring intricate designs sewn with multi-coloured threads. The decorative tassels, bells, and beads adorned it, producing a melodic symphony with every step of the camel. A garland of trinkets and dry flowers adorned the camel's neck, infusing the arid landscape with vibrancy and fragrance. The camel boasted a well-maintained, lustrous skin, speaking volumes of the pride and care taken by its keeper.

Neelam dismounted and allowed the camel to graze before sitting with a simple stringed instrument at the water's edge. Lost in her musical reverie, she began strumming the instrument, her beauty accentuated by her earth-toned attire. The serene beauty of the lake, with its tales of ancient empires and captivating twilights, added to the enchantment of the scene.

Prince Bhanwar's approach reverberated softly through the air as the gravel crunched beneath his every step, announcing his presence to her. Startled, Neelam briefly glanced up from her instrument, but any tension dissolved as he settled beside her, completely enthralled by her enchanting presence. At that moment, their silence became a reassuring companion, punctuated only by the gentle water lapping against the shore.

As Prince Bhanwar approached her, he was captivated by her radiant glow, like a moth drawn to a flame. He settled at a whisper's distance, inexorably drawn to her magnetic presence. The air was saturated with the heady fragrance of jasmine and the distant calls of peacocks serenading the approaching dusk. On the horizon, the last embers of the setting sun blazed, casting a golden veil over the dunes of the Thar Desert as if whispering the secrets of ancient caravans.

Neelam's initial surprise melted into serene surrender as they shared the silence, a sacred connection punctuated only by her haunting lullaby and the gentle ballet of water embracing the shore. The lake, a true gem of the desert, mirrored the fiery sky while lotuses bobbed gently on the surface, their delicate pink petals unfurling like the day's final prayer.

"Fear not, for I am merely a humble prince," he declared, his voice a warm breeze, his arms outstretched in a gesture of vulnerable peace. His hand brushed against a fallen branch, capturing Neelam's gaze with a playful flourish. In hushed reverence, he vowed, "Enchanting nymph, before the heavens, should this bough be my quiver's kin, I vow." With a decisive crack, the branch surrendered as Bhanwar broke it forcefully, "The hunt shall no longer be my sport." His vulnerability in giving up his sport for her stirred a sense of empathy in Neelam.

Her amazement was evident. A hint of warmth softened her caution as she gazed into the his eyes. The seriousness of a Rajput prince giving up weapons and abandoning age-old customs filled the air, as accurate as the mist rising from the lake.

"Neelam's voice echoed like a symphony created from the whispers of the wind and the rustling leaves, blending into the chorus as she spoke. "This lake tells its story, you see," she explained, "a tale that moves with the turning of the earth."

He was captivated by every detail of her – the gentle slope of her cheek and the cascading locks framing her face like a masterpiece. "And today's verse?" he inquired, his words as soft as the silk of her outfit.

She pondered, her gaze lost in the horizon, painted in hues of amber and rose. "It croons of yearning," she revealed. "Of passions once adrift, now anchored. Of oaths murmured over the embrace of nocturnal tides."

He leaned in, his voice a tender caress, the warmth of his breath mingling with the evening air. "What if I confessed," he breathed, "my pilgrimage here was for enlightenment? That within these waters lies the compass to my soul's uncharted depths?"

Her chuckle was a melody as delicate as the first blush of dawn encircling them. "Prince Bhanwar," she teased, "the lake merely mirrors the essence it beholds."

His eyes never left hers. "And if my essence," he bared his heart, "is a maelstrom of warring tides? If honour and longing duel within me?"

Neelam's eyes locked with his. "Then," she counselled, "you must master the tempest. To seek the eye where calm reigns sovereign."

He reached for her hand, marvelling at the life-affirming heat and subtle strength in her fingers. "Might I implore," he entreated, "for your wisdom? For a refrain to quell the disquiet of my spirit?"

Her grin heralded the dawn of hope, her teeth flashing like lightning in the gathering dusk. "Prince Bhanwar," she proclaimed, "affection is an orchestra. It demands rehearsal, forbearance, and the bravery to heed its call."

And so, they remained, two spirits nestled by a secluded spring, entwined in the rhythm of their united pulse. The lake, a custodian of their developing bond, cradled its confidences.

Prince Bhanwar reclined, the earth's cool breath soothing his skin. "Neelam," he ventured, "do you trust in destiny?"

She thought, her head tilting like a blossom towards the sun. "Destiny," she contemplated, "is akin to the zephyr – it sculpts our voyage, yet we command the helm."

His laughter was a sonnet. "A lyrical retort. Yet, have you ever sensed its sculpting hand?"

"Once," she confided, "in my youth, my matriarch spoke of an omen—a harmony to reshape our existence."

Their gazes intertwined. "Do you hold faith in it?"

She wavered. "I've yearned," she murmured, "for a gaze – for that harmony. But perchance, it's merely a fable."

"Never," he assured, "more than a fable. I've encountered murmurs of a prince searching for verity, wandering these shores, besieged by enigmas."

Her eyes grew wide. "You?"

He affirmed, "I am burdened with secrets," he conceded, "obligations that loom over me. Yet, upon hearing your canticle, Neelam, it seemed fate conspired in our union."

She drew near. "What is it you seek, Prince Bhanwar?"

He paused, then unveiled tales of strife and shattered vows. "I seek absolution," he professed. "A path to venerate my forebears while not echoing their follies."

Neelam's touch paused in the air. "And what if," she breathed, "our songs intertwine? What if your salvation is woven within my melodies?"

He extended his hand, pausing with due reverence. "Then," he avowed, "I shall chase your harmony, even should it lead me past empires and dogmas."

Her smile bloomed once more, signalling a fresh start. As she gazed across the peaceful green shores of the lake, her presence filled the prince with newfound courage and tranquillity, allowing their gentle conversation to flow. Unbeknownst to her, a genuine longing had been sparked within him, its nature mysterious and puzzling. There they lingered—a pair by the water's edge—sharing stories and weaving dreams. The lake, a silent witness, reflected their softly spoken confidences. Destiny, much like an approaching storm, is observed from a distance.

In the following days, Prince Bhanwar made deliberate efforts to spend time with Neelam. Chief Nagarmal, the respected leader and protector of their Banjara tribe, felt a persistent apprehension as he observed the notable increase in their interactions. He doubted the prince's motives and apparent affection for his daughter. Renowned for his astute insights into the dynamics of budding relationships among the youth, Chief Nagarmal trusted his instincts, which suggested that the connection he witnessed between Neelam and the Prince was not just temporary; it had the intensity of an emerging blaze, capable of creating immense joy, like diamonds, or causing ruinous destruction.

Nagarmal faced the delicate task of approaching the prince without stirring up hatred or disrespect between their families. After some thought, he invited the prince to join him on a pilgrimage to a sacred temple revered by the Banjaras. Predictably, the prince respectfully declined, stating that his Rajput pride would not allow him to worship at the temple of a different clan.

Nagarmal chose his moment carefully to address the prince, raising a significant concern troubling him. With a firm resolve, he asked, "My Prince, if the strong adherence to Rajput customs hinders you from visiting a temple, how can my daughter form an honourable bond with you? Your dedication to these customs seems to preclude marriage to her. What hope does she have?"

The prince was visibly shaken by Nagarmal's probing inquiry, questioning his devotion to Neelam amidst his cultural obligations. The clash between his desires and the rigid expectations of his Rajput heritage was a source of deep uncertainty, tearing at the fabric of his being.

The prince spent the night wrestling with unease, tormented by the serious considerations brought on by Nagarmal's confrontation. Torn between his heart's desires and his lineage, he contemplated the problematic choice before him. At dawn, the Prince and Neelam met at the riverbank, bathed in the ethereal glow of the rising sun. Prince Bhanwar took Neelam's hands in his, looking into her eyes with unwavering ardour, his profound love for her emanating from his gaze.

"My love for you transcends all boundaries. I would relinquish my kingdom, power, and stature to have you by my side as my wife," he declared with unwavering devotion.

Neelam, her composure steadfast, sternly countered his impassioned declaration. "You cannot forsake all that you hold dear – your family, your duties, and your people," she asserted, gesturing towards his entourage and the opulent tent behind him.

But the prince, resolute in his determination, stepped forward. He took Neelam's hands in his, his resolve unshaken. "I am prepared to leave behind everything I have ever known. I will depart from my father's palace and renounce all that ties me, but I cannot imagine a life without you as my wife," he declared, his words echoing with his unwavering commitment.

Neelam was overwhelmed with joy as her emotions surged like a storm, flooding every fibre with unrestrained euphoria. In that fleeting moment, the world around them faded insignificance as they found solace in each other's embrace, enveloped in pure, unadulterated bliss.

As they returned to the Banjara village in the soft moonlight after their secret meeting in the peaceful forest, an air of anticipation filled the atmosphere. Surprised by their sudden appearance, the villagers gathered in hushed awe, their whispers spreading like wildfire. The prince, exuding confidence, guided Neelam to Chief Nagarmal's residence, with her by his side every step. Each glance and every touch spoke volumes about his love for her. Neelam followed his every step, a testament to her unwavering determination to declare her love for Prince Bhanwar.

Approaching the chief's house, the waft of wood smoke and aromatic spices mingled with the distant melodies and laughter from the village huts. The villagers gaped in disbelief as the Prince and Neelam weaved through the crowd, their fingers intertwined, their hearts beating as one. Finally, they arrived at the chief's doorstep.

The chief emerged and summoned the village elders for a solemn discussion with the young couple. The chief then addressed the prince, seated amongst the elders, his countenance grave.

"My Prince, is this how you repay my hospitality? Daring to parade through my village and arrive at my doorstep, hand in hand with my daughter, in full public view. What are your intentions here?"

Bhanwar, with folded hands and a severe demeanour, cut to the chase without preamble or hesitation.

"I seek your blessing to marry your exquisite daughter."

The chief's visage twisted with a mixture of shock and disapproval. Deep down, however, he understood that this development was inevitable. After a tense silence, he responded calmly, his words carrying the weight of his disapproval.

"No, this cannot be. It is not right," he declared firmly, briefly pausing. "Your father will never approve. We cannot allow this to happen. A prince marrying a Banjara girl will only ruin us all." The chief's words hung heavy in the air, a stark reminder of the societal repercussions of their love.

Bhanwar's grip on Neelam's hand tightened as he spoke, his determination unwavering.

"Sir, I will marry Neelam, even if my father does not approve or bless our union. I can endure losing my kingdom and title, but I cannot bear to see my future wife lose her father's love." Bhanwar's grip on Neelam's hand tightened as he spoke, his determination unwavering, a testament to the depth of his love and the strength of his resolve.

The chief stood up, his face clouded with confusion and concern.

"My Prince, please do not push this any further.

Only suffering can come from it,"

Bhanwar stood his ground, his voice unwavering and resolute.

"I choose this path, no matter the consequences. I will stay here in this humble village, even if it means a life of servitude with the gipsy folk in your clan, the Banjara community. No storm or obstacle can sway my heart from Neelam's."

The chief's shoulders sagged in resignation as he realised nothing could change the prince's mind. "May the gods have mercy on you both," he said solemnly, yet a smile played at the edges of his lips, and a quivering moustache added evidence of the subtle joy he felt.

His hands still shook as he held his head in disbelief. He was sure Bhanwar's father, King Balchand, would never agree. Nagarmal feared him, as the man had immense power that could be used to destroy their entire village as punishment for this act.

As the sun dipped below the horizon, casting an ethereal golden glow over the village, Bhanwar turned to Nagarmal with an intense and heartfelt plea. Amidst the time-worn sandstone structures and the timeless expanse of the desert, he implored the revered village priest to partake in an impromptu and clandestine ceremony, a union that could not wait.

Urgency permeated the air as Bhanwar swiftly directed one of his trusted men to gallop to the distant royal palace, bearing a fabricated tale of prolonged hunting expeditions to justify his absence and ensure the postponement of the impending marriage ceremony. This deception was vital for Bhanwar to clandestinely unite with his beloved Neelam, defying the constraints imposed by tradition and duty. Despite the unease lingering in the atmosphere, Neelam's heart overflowed with joy, though shadowed by underlying apprehensions. Ultimately, it was the genuine desires of their hearts that emerged triumphant.

"Amidst the fading embrace of the sunlight, our celebration shall unfurl," Nagarmal proclaimed, fully aware of the profound auspiciousness associated with weddings conducted under the watchful gaze of the stars.

Despite the limited time for preparation, the close-knit village community ensured that the festivities came together seamlessly, much like a synchronised flight of birds across the vast desert sky.

The desert hamlet was full of life as townsfolk gathered, their garments vibrant against the arid sands. The prince walked to the front, speaking in hushed tones that seemed to signal the arrival of rain. A deep sense of respect and eager anticipation filled the square. Dressed in regal crimson and gold, the prince exuded an aura of allure and poise. His headgear was adorned with an elegant plume and pearls, and his blade, a symbol of nobility and courage, shimmered in the fading daylight.

In front of him was a stage covered in colourful fabrics, ready to receive the holy fire. It was where wedding rituals would unite two destinies under the guidance of the officiant. The area was adorned with flowers and fragrant decorations, creating a joyful atmosphere for the upcoming union.

At the Prince's side, the bride radiated a unique blend of elegance and strength, capturing the attention of everyone around her. Like mirrors reflecting the morning dew, her eyes sparkled as if they were competing with the stars scattered across the blue sky.

Her skin, touched by the gentle night breeze, glowed with the love bestowed by Bhanwar. Draped in luxurious scarlet silk, her gown whispered ancestral tales of devotion and age-old legacies, with every stitch telling a story.

Adorned with henna, her hands carried the ancient stories of banyan roots. Her jewellery reflected a natural radiance that captivated observers, adding to the ceremonial elegance. The prince and the radiant bride locked eyes as they listened to the sacred verses recited by the esteemed priest, the words casting a spell over the holy event. Their clasped hands represented a shared rhythm, each step toward the fire shaping the resonance of their vows. Making seven circles around the blaze, each turn symbolising a heartfelt promise, they stepped into a new chapter driven by enduring love and faithfulness. The bride's laughter, reminiscent of a peacock's call, filled the air with joyful anticipation. The assembled guests recognised this bond as transcending worldly boundaries, celebrating the enduring power of love.

As the Prince applied the vermilion crest upon her brow, marking their paths intertwining, it seemed as if the moon bathed them in a gentle radiance, adding a touch of the sublime to their commitment. Their exchanged glances silently testified to a unity that surpassed royalty, a tale of intertwined souls forever inscribed in the annals of time's desert canvas. The crowd's ecstatic cheers reverberated around them, echoing like the roar of approaching rains, heralding the triumph of love over outdated customs.

In this spiritual union, the Prince beheld the uncharted depths of her spirit and professed his undying loyalty. There she stood, the bride—stately and radiant—a formidable yet delicate embodiment of Rajasthan's soul, enchanting all under the spellbinding lunar orb.

Chapter 5:

Till Death Do Us Part

"I loved her - love will find its way."

Through paths where wolves would fear to prey;

And if it dares enough, 'there hard.

If passion met not some reward,

No matter how, or where, or why,

I did not vainly seek, nor sigh:

Yet sometimes, with remorse, in vain.

I wish she had not loved again.

She died. I dare not tell thee how;

But look, 'tis written on my brow!

– The Giaour by Lord Byron

For six months, Prince Bhanwar was consumed by love and wove a tangled web of deception to shield his forbidden affection for Neelam. Each passing day became a gruelling struggle as he fabricated reports for his regal parents, pretending to be busy hunting and exploring their modest realm.

Concealed beneath the facade of a devoted son, Bhanwar's heart quivered with unease, knowing that his intricate charade could not endure indefinitely. The weight of his falsehoods grew increasingly burdensome, laden with the inevitable disappointment and fury that would ensue.

As rumours of the prince's clandestine union with Neelam permeated the discontented ranks, the soldiers seethed with resentment towards the prince's duplicity, seeking to evade their obligations. They had been mere pawns in a game between father and son, leaving their kin behind to enact Bhanwar's subterfuge.

The news of Prince Bhanwar's involvement with Neelam inevitably reached King Balchand Bhati and Queen Vanshikha. The shock that spread throughout the kingdom foreshadowed impending troubles for all involved. Tension filled the air as the consequences of Bhanwar's choices darkened their once-tranquil kingdom.

King Balchand Bhati sat rigidly on his throne, his expression unreadable, while the courtiers waited anxiously. Beside him, Queen Vanshikha's gaze betrayed the turmoil she felt inside. The court's unity was shattered as some quietly supported the prince's pursuit of love while others whispered about obligations and the challenge to established customs.

Her son's actions disheartened Queen Vanshikha, but she ultimately found it in her heart to forgive him for marrying beneath his station, showing the depth of her maternal compassion. Meanwhile, King Balchand reacted with fury. He sought solace from his most trusted adviser, the family priest, lamenting how his son's impulsive decisions had tarnished his good name and reputation.

The elderly priest sat silently, his wise eyes fixed on the king as he pondered the weighty issue. After a moment, he spoke in a calm but resolute voice.

"Your Highness, the current situation poses a grave threat to the stability of your reign. The prince, young and impressionable, appears to have fallen under the spell of the Banjara woman. You must take swift and decisive action to assert your authority and remind all that you are the ruler, and your word is law, even to your son."

King Balchand absorbed the gravity of the priest's words, acknowledging their wisdom. "I believe you are right," he replied thoughtfully. What do you suggest we do?"

The priest leaned forward slightly; his tone measured but adamant. "I propose that you engage Bhanwar in a conversation, clarifying that while he may continue his relationship with the woman, marriage is not an option. Instead, he will be promptly betrothed to the daughter of a prominent leader. This will allow him to fulfil his desires while upholding the dignity of our family."

King Balchand understood that protecting his reputation and authority was crucial. Despite being concerned about his son's potential distress, he knew it was necessary to take decisive action to uphold the honour of their dynasty. With a solemn nod, the king agreed to the priest's counsel.

He informed Queen Vanshikha of his plan to summon their son home and implement the priest's recommendations by riding to meet his son.

"I have devoted my life to serving you," she replied fearfully, her words hesitant, knowing her husband's unpredictable temper. "I will always put your interests above mine or our children's." Her hands trembled slightly as she spoke, a sign of her nervousness.

"Before you depart to meet the prince, please consider and evaluate his sincere and enduring feelings for this Banjara woman. We should contemplate the possibility of bringing her into our home if his emotions are more than just infatuation,"

Balchand's piercing gaze narrowed into a withering glare, one that could stop a charging elephant in its tracks. The queen, caught off guard by the sudden malice behind his eyes, could only flinch as she was struck by a sharp slap that sent her reeling. A metallic tang filled her mouth as she tasted the blood trickling from the corner of her lips.

Breathless, disappointed and shaken, Queen Vanshikha watched her husband storm out of the room. His booming voice demanded his horse be brought to him, and with an entourage of soldiers following closely behind, he galloped towards the Banjara village. He was confident that his son was cavorting with his forbidden lover there.

As the echoes of his rage faded into the distance, a heavy pall of gloom descended upon the palace, mirroring the queen's fears for what horrors her husband's unchecked wrath may unleash. A sense of foreboding hung thick in the air, suffocating everyone within the palace walls.

As the first light of dawn gently spread across the sky, it bathed Balchand and his tired platoon of warriors in a soft, amber glow as they approached the peaceful Banjara village. Despite their exhausting night, their unwavering spirit pushed them forward.

As they neared the Banjara abode, King Balchand noticed the camp of the prince's forces. They dismounted from their steeds, and with determined expressions, Balchand sought information about Prince Bhanwar. He was told that the prince lived in the heart of the Banjara settlement with his consort, Neelam, in a charming cottage within the hamlet. This revelation led to a frown of annoyance on Balchand's face. Gathering his resolve, he ordered his men to arm themselves, and with purposeful strides, they made their way to the unassuming village.

They were approached by Nagarmal, the respected chieftain of the Banjara clan, who welcomed them warmly and invited them into his humble home. One of Balchand's battle-hardened soldiers recognised Nagarmal and revealed his identity. When Balchand realised they were in the presence of the woman's father who had captured his son's heart, his face contorted with anger. Overcome by rage, he lunged forward and pushed Nagarmal to the ground in spite.

"Where is my son?" he demanded, his voice thundering. "Is he revelling in the luxuries of your unsuitable daughter?"

Struggling to his feet, Nagarmal responded with desperate sincerity. "My esteemed king, your son has willingly wedded my daughter. They have chosen to embark on a new journey together. I implore you to embrace my daughter as your own."

But Balchand dismissed Nagarmal's plea. He spat disdainfully in Nagarmal's direction and bellowed, "Summon my son and his so-called wife here at this instant! I am determined to retrieve my son!"

The Banjara chief shook his head sorrowfully. "My king," he implored calmly, "please compose yourself." With a respectful bow, he added, "I will bring them here promptly. But I urge you to accept your son's selection of my daughter as his bride."

The sun's warm embrace painted the charming cabin by the tranquil lake, casting a golden glow upon its wooden walls. Vivid and alive blooming flowers framed this idyllic scene, while verdant plants whispered secrets to the breeze. Towering hills draped in ancient forests stood sentinel in the distant backdrop. A lone villager hurried along the well-trodden earthen paths, their steps echoing softly. The urgency in his gait matched the weight of the message. The messenger reached the Prince's abode, its doorway adorned with intricate carvings, and knocked with a fervour born of great importance.

"My Prince, my Prince!" the villager called out, breathless. "Your father has arrived, and his mood is foul. Nagarmal, Neelam's father, summons you to assuage King Balchand's wrath."

The prince emerged from the cabin, his robe trailing behind him like a comet's tail. Neelam, her eyes wide with fear and longing, stepped forward. "Stay," she pleaded, her voice a fragile whisper. "Vanish with me into the forest, away from duty and strife."

The prince was resolute in his decision. He looked into Neelam's eyes, his gaze reflecting the soft white light of a passing cloud. "I cannot," he said, his voice filled with responsibility. "We cannot flee; we must face this clash head-on."

With a lingering touch, he left Neelam standing by the cabin, torn between love and duty. As he walked towards the waiting horse, he carried the burden of his princely title and the pain of a love that could never be fully realised. The sun dipped lower, casting long shadows across the path as the prince rode towards the clearing.

Neelam's face expressed sorrow and determination as she watched the prince leave. Her eyes glistened as she traced his departure. Gripping her ornate shawl, her hands shook with love and yearning, leaving their mark on her tender face. As the daylight dimmed and touched her visage, deep sadness was etched in the shadows it created. Sensing an unspoken dread, she abruptly followed Bhanwar's departing trail. He glanced over his shoulder and turned his steed back to her. Noting her turmoil, he said nothing but gently lifted her onto his horse. Together, they rode on towards the impending confrontation.

Upon Bhanwar's arrival, anger contorted Balchand's face when he saw his son with Neelam. His hands balled into fists at the sight of them, hand in hand, and he growled fiercely.

"This temptress has tricked you. It's a shame that my son has been so naive! Haven't I taught you anything? Being a man means having a lover! You will consider this woman your pleasure, but I will arrange a marriage with a maiden worthy of your companionship, both by blood and her father's riches."

The prince pleaded for forgiveness, but his father remained unmoved. His gaze turned towards Neelam, filled with scorn.

"Neelam," he paused for emphasis and continued, "your father named you aptly after a precious stone. Sapphire is a fitting name for a gold-digger like you. Women like you can be bought with just a few coins."

His words dripped with contempt and disgust, breaking Neelam's gentle heart as she had come to her father-in-law with the faint hope of reconciliation. Balchand's contemptuous words hung heavily in the air.

Prince Bhanwar's voice remained steady, a thin veil of control masking the storm within. "Father," he began, "if you cannot accept me or my love for Neelam, then I shall never return to the palace. I willingly forgo the right to call myself a Prince or your son. You go your way, and I shall go mine."

His words hung in the air, a challenge flung across the chasm that divided them. Balchand's face contorted with rage, and he pivoted towards Neelam, his fingers curling around the hilt of a golden dagger. With a swift motion, he flung it at her feet, a glittering testament to his wrath.

"This," he thundered, "is more than you and your wretched father will ever earn in your worthless lifetime." The dagger quivered in the earth, its blade catching the fading sunlight.

Neelam stood her ground, unyielding. Balchand's threat was a storm, but she was the rooted tree. Her voice, surprisingly steady, cut through the tension. "If this is your attempt to buy my love for your son," she said, "know that it can never be bought. Love is not a commodity, nor can it be bartered."

Balchand's face flushed crimson, anger boiling within him. Neelam met his gaze, her eyes unwavering. Her courage mingled with quiet grace, a dance of defiance. Balchand recognised the same fire that had once burned in his veins. He broke their gaze, stepping away as if seeking refuge from the truth.

But then he turned back, scanning Neelam's face as if searching for something beyond defiance. His voice softened to a mere echo of the storm. "I offer you one final chance," he said.

Neelam's reply was fierce, her spirit unyielding. "Your words," she declared, "are nothing but hollow promises. My love for your son transcends wealth and power. It is woven into the very fabric of my being—a tapestry that no dagger, no threat can tear asunder."

Balchand's response was a thunderous roar of anger that echoed through the clearing, sending chills down the spines of all who heard it. His eyes blazed with fury as he lunged forward, snatching the sword from one of his guards with a swift, practised motion. The glinting metal caught the light, casting ominous reflections as it arced towards Nagarmal, who was desperately pleading for forgiveness for his daughter and son-in-law. Nagarmal, believing he could mediate between the two parties, dared to step forward, his hands raised in a gesture of peace.

With a vicious snarl, Balchand brought the blade down upon Nagarmal's right arm with the force of a bolt of lightning. Blood sprayed in all directions as three fingers were severed cleanly when the sword tore through Nagarmal's palm. The once-pristine ground glistened red with fresh blood, but Balchand showed no remorse. The sight of the blood seemed to enrage him even further. His wild eyes, filled with a terrifying intensity, locked onto Nagarmal as he raised his blood-stained weapon, advancing as if to finish him off.

Suddenly, however, Balchand changed course maliciously. With a cruel twist of his lips, he spun towards Neelam, his intentions clear.

Bhanwar's heart sank as he saw his father heading straight for his beloved Neelam. Without hesitation, he rushed forward to protect her, but Balchand was faster than expected. With a quick swing of his sword, he caught Bhanwar mid-stride, and the sword's hilt collided with Bhanwar's face with brutal force.

Bhanwar stumbled to his knees, weakened and disoriented from the blow. Blood poured from his nose and mouth as he knelt on the ground, helpless against his own father's wrath. Two screams pierced the air - one from Neelam as her hair dragged her away and the other from Queen Vanshikha, who had just arrived at the unfolding calamity. Her worst fears were realised as she saw her son hurt by his enraged father. The queen's scream was a mix of horror and desperation, her eyes wide with disbelief as she rushed forward, her heart pounding in her chest.

Balchand's grip on Neelam's hair tightened as he dragged her across the clearing, his eyes never leaving Bhanwar's. "This is what happens when you defy me!" he roared, his voice echoing through the trees. Neelam's cries of pain and fear filled the air, but Balchand seemed deaf to her pleas. His focus was solely on inflicting as much pain and suffering as possible.

Queen Vanshikha reached Bhanwar's side, her hands trembling as she tried to help him to his feet.

"We must stop him," she whispered urgently, her voice breaking. "He'll kill her."

Bhanwar, still dazed from the blow, nodded weakly. He struggled to stand, his legs shaking beneath him. "We have to save her," he gasped, his voice filled with determination despite his injuries.

Together, they moved towards Balchand, their hearts heavy with fear and resolve. The clearing was filled with the sounds of their struggle, the clash of metal, and the cries of the wounded. It was a scene of chaos and violence, a testament to the destructive power of unchecked rage.

Amid turmoil and aggression, Bhanwar noticed something shining. It was the golden dagger Balchand had presented to Neelam, attempting to win her affection for his son. Battling through agony and distress, Bhanwar extended his hand to seize the dagger, imploring his ruthless father for mercy. Yet, Balchand's desire for retribution appeared unquenchable.

"Father, you've rejected me and scorned my love. You may be entitled to that, but I'll always acknowledge Neelam," Prince Bhanwar proclaimed, his voice shaking with feeling in front of King Balchand, his father.

Queen Vanshikha ran to her son's side, tears streaming down her face, as she faced the enraged Balchand and pleaded for mercy. Her hands trembled as she reached out to touch her son's bloodied face and begged him to reconsider.

Balchand remained unmoved by the scene of his injured son and the laments of his wife. His grip on Neelam's hair remained tight and cruel. His eyes burned with fury as he looked at his son with disdain.

"My Lord, enough of this," Queen Vanshikha desperately cried out. "Let us leave this place at once! Our son has made a mistake, and you have already punished him. Please, let us return to the palace; I beg you, do not do anything that would bring us further sorrow!"

Balchand stood firm, his anger boiling over at his son's betrayal. He spat out harsh, venomous words aimed at Bhanwar.

"You, my flesh and blood, dare challenge me for this woman. Your moral compass has failed you disastrously. You lost all rights to be considered my son." His tone dripped with venom and disappointment. Their relationship as father and son was shattered beyond repair.

Balchand turned his gaze towards Neelam, slumped on the ground, trying weakly to escape his vice-like grip on her hair. With a rage-filled roar, he raised his sword to her throat.

In an instant, Prince Bhanwar ran forward, screaming desperately. "No, Father! Do not do this!"

Balchand pointed his sword towards him, stopping him from getting any closer. He glowered at Neelam as she attempted to break free and escape to Bhanwar's outstretched arms. Suddenly, her tangled tresses slipped from Balchand's fingers. Seeing her move closer to Bhanwar, he bellowed an order to a soldier nearby.

"Break her leg so that she cannot run away!"

Without hesitation, the soldier brandished his heavy spear and swung it deftly. The heavy shaft landed with a vicious thud on the ball of her ankle, shattering it and allowing bone to break through her skin. She hit the ground hard and crashed down into the sand. Her eyes watered as she looked down in disbelief at her delicate foot, now dangled at an impossible angle, broken beyond repair. Blood gushed from between her pale fingers, which were trying to hold the mangled mess together, and then an immense, mind-numbing pain coursed through Neelam's being. She screamed in anguish, face down in the dirt.

She paled as a giddiness overtook her. She groaned and looked up in anguish through watery eyes. Balchand had moved between her and his son. He pointed his sword at her and thundered at the Prince, who had moved purposefully toward Neelam to protect her from further harm. "Stand your ground, or I will have the life ripped out of this wretched creature right here!"

The prince paused, overwhelmed by the disarray that lay before him. What had been a tranquil encampment was now marred by disorder and misfortune.

Observing her husband overwhelmed by anger, Queen Vanshikha's maternal instincts surged to

the forefront. She tried to move towards Neelam but was held back by Balchand's soldiers. As she struggled against their grip, she stumbled and fell hard, knocking the breath out of her and leaving her speechless and immobilised.

Observing the cruelty on display, Bhanwar realised that things were out of control. With a heavy heart and a voice filled with pain, he addressed his father.

"Father, today you stand as a king, not a parent. Your verdict has forsaken the ties of our kinship. Although I have lost your presence today, I still wish to preserve my bond with my mother. And living without Neelam is beyond my endurance. There exists but a sole path to her salvation," he halted briefly, eyes locking with Neelam's, and murmured gently, "Grant me pardon in our present days. Embrace me in the lifetime that follows."

Neelam's heart skipped a beat as she heard the cold melancholy resonating in the prince's words. With all his might, he brought it slicing downward, piercing through flesh and bone until it reached his beating heart. A near-silent hiss escaped his lips. Blood gushed freely, and the crimson stain grew. With each heartbeat, his life slipped away, stepping towards oblivion.

Amidst the chaos and anguish, Balchand rushed over to his son's side, roaring in agony. "No! What have you done?"

Bhanwar's eyes flickered, the light fading as quickly as his remaining moments on earth. The dagger had found its mark and remained faithful to its forger's intent.

Seeing all this, Neelam was caught up in a frenzy. She attempted to hobble towards her collapsed lover, but her mangled foot made each step agonisingly painful. She collapsed and dragged herself towards Bhanwar.

Balchand, consumed by rage and grief, snarled at a nearby soldier. "Stop her!"

The soldier moved forward with a murderous intent, tightening his grip on Neelam's arm. The prince understood that time was running out before his love would be ripped away forever.

Overcome with urgency, Neelam mustered her last bit of energy and screamed as she tried to reach her beloved. She struggled against the soldier's firm hold, scratching at his arm and yearning to hold Bhanwar close as his life faded away. She pulled away and fell at Bhanwar's side. She held his hand, but there was no response. Bhanwar's eyes were shut tight. His breathing laboured. However, the soldier was unyielding, and within moments, Neelam was forcibly separated, reaching out for her love, whose life was slipping away slowly but surely.

The prince gazed at Neelam with sorrowful eyes and whispered dejectedly, "We will meet again. I promise." And with those words, his outstretched arms relaxed, and he passed away.

Balchand let out a heart-wrenching howl at the sight of his son's lifeless body.

Neelam seethed with rage. She had come within inches of holding Bhanwar's head in his last moments. She screamed maniacally. She had paid the ultimate price for love.

"Oh, king by title alone, today you upheld your ancestors' customs but betrayed human decency. What was your son's crime? What was mine? Is this justice? What about the fairness you guarantee your people? Where was the safeguarding you pledge to your realm's inhabitants?"

She stopped, struggling to catch her breath as she pulled herself up with trembling arms only to stumble back to the ground as her broken leg failed her. Looking down at her hands, she saw the red stains from Bhanwar's lifeless body, the stickiness a harsh reminder of the tragedy. A wave of sadness and regret overcame her, causing her to close her eyes and silently pray for his departed soul. However, when she opened her eyes again, a strong surge of anger swept over her, igniting a chilling, high-pitched scream that echoed through the eerie, desolate surroundings. The sound lingered like a vengeful ghost, unsettling anyone who dared to listen. With fingers-stained crimson, she expressed her lament, casting accusatory glances toward Bhanwar's evil father, the wicked Balchand.

"I curse you and all future generations of your bloodline! May you suffer and waste until your dying breath, never finding peace or redemption for your actions today. May the fate of your male descendants be no different, doomed to suffer until they die in the most horrific ways imaginable."

Neelam used the edge of her garment to wipe away the crimson mark on her forehead, erasing the symbol of her broken marriage – a sign she no longer deserved as a widow. Her trembling fingers, filled with a mix of rage and sorrow, unintentionally smudged Bhanwar's blood across her face as she removed the dignified emblem.

The realisation that Bhanwar's blood marked her skin made her let out a savage cry that sent paralysing shivers through the onlookers. The raw ferocity of her lamentation cut through the silence, unsettling even the most steadfast warriors as she cursed the fates.

Neelam's madness was rising. She rambled incoherently but with sufficient clarity to strike fear in those who watched and listened.

"Let the very fabric of existence tremble at my invocation, for I weave curses with threads of cosmic wrath. Listen to the words that echo from the abyss, their syllables etched in blood and fire. May the earth beneath your feet scorn your presence, its soil turning barren and bleak. Let roots writhe and twist away from your touch, denying sustenance to any life that dares to grow near you. The sun shall shun your shadow, casting long, cold fingers across your path, a perpetual eclipse of hope.

The cries of your forebears, those who once bore your name, shall haunt your nights. Their voices, spectral and mournful, will pierce your dreams like shards of shattered glass.

I cast this dire hex upon the winds of fate, binding it to the very marrow of your bones. A malevolent spectre shall linger over your lineage through the aeons. Your sons, those unwitting bearers of your tainted legacy, shall inherit not riches or honour but a legacy of suffering. Their footsteps shall echo in desolate halls, their laughter swallowed by the void.

Let each heartbeat of your progeny be a drumbeat of anguish. Their joys shall curdle into bitterness, their triumphs into ashes. Love will elude them like a phantom, slipping through their fingers as they reach for it. Their eyes shall mirror your own—haunted, hollow, and ever-yearning for redemption.

As you draw your final, ragged breath, may the spectre of desolation cling to you. It will wrap around your chest, squeezing out the last vestiges of warmth. No priest's absolution, no tearful confession, shall lift this curse. You shall die alone, abandoned by gods and men alike, your soul a shipwreck on the shores of eternity.

And when your name is whispered in hushed tones, it will carry the weight of tragedy. 'Balchand,' they'll say, 'the cursed one.' Your memory shall be a cautionary tale, a caution against hubris, against cruelty, against the folly of believing oneself above consequence.

So go forth, Balchand, with your ill-gotten wealth and tarnished honour. Walk your chosen path, but know this: the shadows trail behind you, hungry for retribution. And when the final chapter of your story is written, it shall be inked in blood, illuminated by the dying embers of regret."

Her words were ominous. Balchand hesitated, but his anger stifled the fear that had started creeping up his spine. With a final burst of rage, Balchand barked orders to his men.

"Take that witch away from here," he spat, his face contorted with fury. "Bury her somewhere where no one can find her. Let her suffer a slow, agonising death, alone with her regret and grief. She deserves nothing less for the pain she has caused me and my family."

As the soldiers dragged Neelam away, her eyes were blank and empty, frozen in a state of shock. Despite her terrible condition, she continued to curse Balchand's family between high-pitched wails.

"What pain can you possibly give me?" she screamed, her voice filled with anguish and desperation. "I have seen more pain than any woman should ever endure on God's good earth."

In a single swift movement, she ripped off her glass bangles and flung them to the ground, obliterating any symbol of her married status. Her father, Nagarmal, watched in despair as his daughter discarded all traces of her love for Bhanwar. She was now a widow. The unfairness of the unfolding events ignited Neelam's anger, fuelling her bitter words.

She said viciously, through sobs and tears, "I watched as my husband took his own life right before my eyes. The suffering that you and your loved ones will now face is beyond comprehension. You've ripped me and my yet-to-be-born child away from the man we love. Your family will experience this pain too, and the impact of your actions will be felt for generations."

Queen Vanshikha's heart ached as she listened to Neelam's heartfelt words. She sank to her knees on the rain-soaked ground, not caring about the mud that stained her once pristine white dress. The mention of the unborn child struck her with an overwhelming sense of sadness and loss.

Balchand stood there, unmoving, his usual confidence and poise replaced by a look of utter shock. The self-assured demeanour that had often stirred envy in others had vanished as he confronted the grave consequences of his actions. The peaceful and scenic surroundings outside the Banjara village now held the weight of an incomprehensible tragedy.

His once steady hands now trembled at his sides, gripped by disbelief and horror. He had never imagined the extent of devastation his carelessness could cause until this moment. The tragedy of a life lost before it could even begin weighed heavily on him, leaving him frozen in body and speech.

There seemed to be no room for regret or redemption. The irreversible repercussions permanently damaged the kingdom's future and the royal lineage. As Balchand grappled with the gravity of his mistake, a sudden downpour broke his train of thought. The rain poured down as if to cleanse the land of the innocent bloodshed, serving as both a literal and symbolic attempt to wash away the deed.

Yet, the downpour also felt like a chilling indictment of Balchand's misdeeds. The coldness of the water seemed to mirror the dread settling in his soul as if nature was emphasising his guilt. Amidst the unrelenting rain, he questioned whether he would ever find peace while bearing the burden of his actions.

Chapter 6:

Someone Must Go To India

"The torment of precautions often exceeds the dangers to be avoided. It is sometimes better to abandon oneself to destiny."

– Napoleon Bonaparte

Candice was utterly engrossed in the story, vividly envisioning the scenes in her mind. She felt a rush of emotion as she pictured Jyoti's unresponsive husband lying in his bed, wishing she knew how to help. Candice willingly followed Jyoti's gesture to enter the living room. They settled comfortably on the couch while an attendant brought snacks and drinks. As they enjoyed the refreshments, Candice sipped her tea but grew restless, tapping her finger on the table.

She knew of the family's troubled past and Jyoti's difficult situation. With politeness, she expressed her reservations about her ability to help. A heavy silence filled the room until Vaibhav softly coughed, bringing Candice's attention back to Jyoti. Candice redirected the conversation and asked about the fate of the Banjara girl and her descendants.

Jyoti shared the sadness of their family history, acknowledging intentional omissions that hindered their understanding of the past. As she recounted the story, Candice focused intently, trying to comprehend the complexities before her. Despite feeling perplexed, she couldn't help but ask, "How can we uncover the truth? How can we possibly unravel all of this?"

Vaibhav nodded thoughtfully and proposed his idea: "The only way to make sense of this is for someone to go to India and collaborate with local experts. We must piece together the puzzle and end this curse that has haunted our family."

Candice couldn't help but scoff at the mention of curses. "Vaibhav, do you truly believe in such things? This is nothing more than an old wives' tale passed down through generations."

However, Jyoti's hands trembled as she reached for a photo album from a stack of nearby documents. Flipping a page, she pointed to pictures of her husband, Avinash, his brother, and his father in succession. She explained.

"How likely would all three of them be affected by the same illnesses? Two of them passed away before turning fifty, and the third is currently on his deathbed. This is unlikely to be connected to an inherited condition or a biological irregularity. Despite seeking insights from top-tier doctors about pathologies and genetic predispositions, modern medical science remains puzzled. The absence of a logical or medical explanation suggests something beyond the natural realm, seemingly supported by Neelam's final words."

Candice seemed disturbed by Jyoti's reference to other family deaths. Jyoti peered intently at Candice, her voice laced with veiled secrets as she spoke.

"Imagine this: What if one of your ancestors left a treasure to you? Wouldn't you want to uncover the mysteries of family history, then?"

Candice's face tightened in mild annoyance. Her cup clattered against the saucer as she set it down. "What are you saying? Is this about a treasure?" she asked cautiously.

Vaibhav answered in a sombre tone. "No, it is about life and death. A treasure, isn't it?"

He waited for Candice to realise the metaphor of a treasure, but no realisation came. He then pulled out a leather-bound chart, which Candice recognised as genealogical.

"The challenge with these charts is that they are great until maybe two hundred years ago; after that, they become patchy."

He put his finger on a name Candice could not read from where she was sitting and continued talking.

"In 1492, Rao Jodha, a descendant of the Rathore clan, founded Jodhpur as detailed in recorded history. They held dominion over various fiefdoms within the Jodhpur region, with kings and chiefs pledging loyalty to them. During that period, Jodhpur's territorial expanse was greater than today's. After India gained independence in 1947, the former royal boundaries and fiefdoms were redefined as constitutional territories by democratic principles. This marked a significant change for the region."

Vaibhav pointed to the family tree, his eyes reflecting the mystery of their past. "My forebears, the Bhatis, governed one of these fiefdoms. Our family's genealogy is well-documented, but information on smaller fiefdoms is sparse or missing unless some investigative work is carried out."

After finishing his sandwich and dusting his hands, he proceeded with the history. "The records we've found allow us to trace our lineage back around two hundred years, but we lack the details to connect us definitively to King Balchand and Prince Bhanwar. Our family history remains an enigmatic puzzle that beckons us towards a path filled with adventure and potential discoveries."

Candice was more engrossed in her sandwich than in the historical tales of Indian cities and royal bloodlines. However, she was keen to be polite to her hosts, so she pressed on. "So, you're unaware of your ancestors. But haven't you considered asking a relative who might appreciate your lineage enough to investigate it?"

Vaibhav responded with a patient smile, "You must realise why we haven't pursued that. The challenge lies in having to undertake this in India, where the person would have to address not just my father's sickness but its underlying cause as well. We are caught in an ongoing battle of emotions, grappling with our history on one hand and our father's wellbeing on the other."

Candice stood up and asked hesitantly, "So now you must find out about your family history and get medical help for your father. But which is more important, finding out about your past or getting him treatment? They do not seem linked, so what should be the priority?"

Vaibhav and his mother appeared perplexed. "This illness isn't related to any physical ailment, Candice. We're certain of that," Jyoti explained. "We believe it's because of the curse uttered by Neelam," she continued, her voice carrying the weight of their conviction. The intensity of our desperation is evident, and our belief in the curse reflects the extremes we're prepared to reach to heal our beloved Avinash."

Candice's body was poised as if in anticipation of an early departure. "Thank you for this conversation," she muttered curtly, "but I'm afraid I'm done here. I'm a lawyer, not a faith healer. The concept or notion of curses is beyond me, and I don't think I should be any part of it." Her professional identity was a shield against the unfamiliar and the unexplainable.

Vaibhav's gaze bore into Candice as he still asked in a low, questioning, yet firm voice, "Candice, will you take this assignment and go to India as a personal favour to my family?"

Silence filled the room as Candice shook her head and pursed her lips. Her response bordered on disbelief, but she bit her tongue out of respect for her association with the Bhati family. She continued slowly to pivot the conversation to something more meaningful. "You mentioned that you want to solve this by going to India. Where in India? And why?"

Vaibhav jumped into the conversation. To help her understand, Vaibhav spread open a large map. The green-brown crescent of a state was printed on top and covered two-thirds of the page.

"This is a map of Rajasthan, my home state in India," he said, touching it and turning it around for Candice to see. He circled the word Rajasthan printed on the map. "The name itself means the state of kings. My family has its roots from here," he pointed out Mandore. "It is a historic place I cannot wait for you to see. It was once ruled by the Rathore who…," he trailed off as he saw the incredulous look on Candice's face. She had stopped listening already, lost in thought and worried about where all this was leading.

"No," she said a bit too forcefully. "I do not believe that this concerns lawyers. What is being asked of me goes beyond the law—it is rooted in, I am afraid, superstition. I am a realist! Vaibhav, you are his son and as smart as I am. Why not you?"

Candice did not pause to allow Vaibhav to respond. Her body was poised, anticipating an early departure. She continued hesitantly, "Thank you for this conversation, but I'm afraid I'm done here. I'm a lawyer, not a faith healer. The concept of curses is beyond me, and I don't think I should be any part of it."

Jyoti clasped her hands even tighter as she smiled encouragingly at Candice, her voice soft but firm.

"Avinash and I believe you would be the perfect person for this job. We need someone who won't take anything in this matter at face value and will look deeper than most others in India. We need a logical thinker to assemble all the pieces and find closure. Vaibhav will be emotionally involved in this, and he needs to keep his hands on the steering wheel of our business empire."

Jyoti stared intently at Candice and then Vaibhav, her dark eyes daring them both to contradict her. Candice's eyes widened in surprise as Jyoti made her request. She shook her head in disagreement, her lips pursed, and her voice terse and unsure.

"I don't think I'm the right person to handle this situation. I don't have first-hand experience with India and don't incorporate God into my daily life, so I'm not sure how I can assist. This seems more like a fanciful notion rather than something based on substance. It feels like embarking on a wild goose chase without substantial basis or logic."

Despite the starkness of Candice's words, Jyoti stood firm and responded calmly but with an urgency laced in every syllable of her response.

"Please, Candice, do you think a dying man would lie to you or make something like this up? He needs an answer and deserves assistance from someone who can approach it scientifically. God has not chosen you for this task. We have. Please do not turn your back on us because of fear or disbelief. Think of this as an extension of the work that you do. This would be a fantastic way to bridge time and build your future pipeline of ad hoc work. Right?"

Candice averted her gaze, struggling to reconcile her mixed feelings about God and her abandonment during her time of need. She remained quiet and cautious, not wanting to cause Jyoti any distress or delve into a topic that brought her anguish.

Perceiving an intensity to Candice's reaction, Jyoti thought about broaching the subject of Candice's faith but decided against it to prevent straying from the main issue. Jyoti's voice carried a hint of sorrow as she aimed to persuade Candice to assist in addressing her husband's fatal illness, hoping to mitigate the inevitability of death.

"As his spouse," she clasped her hands and implored, "please see this as fulfilling the last wish of a man nearing his end. We must honour and act on his requests now rather than after he's gone." Her voice wavered with emotion, and tears welled up in her eyes. Candice was taken aback but kept a composed expression. The older woman wiped away her tears and inhaled deeply before continuing, "At this point, all that remains for him is to wait and hold onto hope."

Candice felt a tinge of guilt, but she could not afford to let her emotions get the better of her. She placed one hand on her forehead to stop thinking for a while. She was starting to feel uncomfortable as she stood there. Sensing a letting down of guard, Jyoti started outlining the next steps.

"We have been in touch with an American expatriate who resides in Jodhpur. He has offered to assist you upon your arrival. His name is Dr. Andrew Gladwell," Jyoti's words came to an abrupt halt as she noticed Candice closing her eyes and sinking into a nearby chair, an expression of disbelief evident on her face and in her body language. Jyoti offered a reassuring smile and drew a chair beside her, determined to alleviate Candice's trepidation. She was eager to immerse Candice in the rich tapestry of India, beginning with the vibrant city of Jodhpur.

Chapter 7:

On a Wing and a Prayer

"We live in a wonderful world of beauty, charm and adventure. Our adventures have no end if we only seek them with open eyes."

– Jawaharlal Nehru

As Candice settled into her aeroplane seat, she let the gentle hum of the engines lull her into a state of serenity. With heavy eyelids, she embraced a meditative calm and acknowledged the mix of trepidation and hope swirling within her as she thought about her upcoming journey to Mumbai.

Swept away by dreams, lulled by the plane's gentle rhythm, the flight attendant's gentle touch and whisper awakened her, indicating they would soon be landing. Groggy but quickly regaining her composure, she welcomed the invigorating refreshment of a beverage and a chilled towel. Her gaze was captivated by the dawn's stunning colours shining through her window.

Memories cascaded, imbuing her with a swell of mixed sentiments. The aching of departure and the exciting propulsion toward her impending journey tugged at her heartstrings. She took a calming inhale to ease the whirlwind of emotions, shouldering aside the persisting uncertainties clouding her mind.

Deciding to shake off the lethargy before her arrival, she meandered towards the restroom. The grand spectacle of an ocean of clouds billowing below, a fleeting sanctuary for her preoccupied spirit, awed her with its beauty.

Candice refreshed herself with a splash of water in the small bathroom. Looking into the mirror, she reflected on the decisions and changes that had brought her to this point. After recharging and preparing herself, she returned to her seat among the passengers with renewed determination.

Descending through the heavens, sights set on India's coastal expanse, she craned for her first glimpse of the approaching terrain. The engine's omnipresent hum was a backdrop to her mounting excitement. Candice leaned into the onset of diverse adventures ahead, facing the unknown with unwavering courage.

The landing at Mumbai airport was uneventful. Passport control moved quickly and effortlessly. Candice watched as the officer stamped her passport with practised ease, waved her through the turnstile, and muttered a practised insincere greeting: "Welcome to India. Have a pleasant stay."

She sighed and slightly nodded before approaching the illuminated 'Exit' signs pointing to the terminal's arrival hall.

Upon entering the arrival area, Candice quickly surveyed the lively and busy scene for her guide. She noticed a man with an eye-catching, colourful turban towering above the rest, who was easily distinguishable, holding up a sign bearing her name. His reassuring grin and poised manner helped ease her apprehension as she approached him. He introduced himself as Shyam Singh, and his confident presence immediately put her at ease.

Shyam took charge of Candice's bags with familiarity and efficiently led the way through the sophisticated layout of the terminal. He seemed to weave through the buzzing crowd with ease, carefully avoiding any unnecessary interactions, which provided Candice with a comforting sense of safety.

"In a short while, we will head to Jodhpur," he announced in slightly accented but impeccable English.

His use of 'Mr. Andrew' instead of 'Mr. Gladwell' immediately made Candice feel more at home in this unfamiliar setting. She followed Shyam's lead, feeling profound gratitude for his reassuring presence.

As they stepped onto the small, chartered plane, Shyam settled into his seat toward the rear while Candice, brimming with anticipation, settled into hers. She retrieved a meticulously detailed map of India and delicately trailed her finger over the expanse of Rajasthan, where Andrew's exclusive resort awaited her arrival. Shyam observed her keenly from a distance, exuding unwavering vigilance. His primary responsibility was to ensure her safe passage to Jodhpur, which he approached with steadfast commitment, imparting a profound sense of care and security.

As the plane gracefully descended towards Jodhpur, Candice leaned closer to the window, eager with anticipation. Below, the city of Jodhpur sprawled out like a mesmerising tapestry, with winding alleyways and houses painted in vibrant shades of electric blue, each hue more dazzling than the last. The imposing Mehrangarh Fort stood regally amidst the landscape, its formidable walls and towering ramparts serving as a stoic sentinel, preserving the rich history and stories of Jodhpur's bygone eras.

Candice's eyes widened in wonder at the breathtaking Umaid Bhawan Palace below. The palace, crafted from radiant golden sandstone, stood proudly on its lofty platform, encircled by manicured grounds, emanating nobility and silent dignity. The sight was a testament to human craftsmanship and architectural grandeur, leaving Candice and the audience in awe.

Candice found herself overwhelmed with breathless excitement. The aerial panorama of Jodhpur unfurled before her, stirring a profound sense of wonder and anticipation within her. The journey ahead promised to be filled with new experiences and cultural discoveries, igniting a sense of excitement in both Candice and the audience.

Upon the aircraft's arrival at the modest airport in Jodhpur, Shyam promptly got off the plane and entered the searing heat. Candice cautiously followed, instantly enveloped by a wave of stifling warmth. She yearned for Johannesburg's wintry briskness in the Southern Hemisphere. She quickly retrieved a pair of oversized sunglasses from her handbag and sought refuge from the scorching, unrelenting sunlight. Seemingly impervious to the oppressive heat, Shyam gestured towards an impeccably sleek, black vehicle parked nearby.

Shyam carefully opened the passenger door for Candice and helped her into the car. He expertly loaded Candice's heavy suitcases into the trunk, ensuring they were secure for the journey ahead. As they set off towards their destination, Candice was captivated by the unrelenting heat and the sun's brilliant glare in the desert region. The landscape appeared desolate, with scarce signs of greenery and vast stretches of barren land unfolding before them.

Shyam shared with Candice that they were fortunate to have witnessed recent rainfall during the Indian monsoon season despite the arid appearance of the surroundings. Candice found this hard to believe, considering the arid terrain around them. She couldn't help but wonder how much drier the area would be during a drought despite having experienced rain.

Nearing the airport's exit, an alert security guard with a firearm meticulously inspected their car. Candice cringed at the gun, but Shyam's assured and amiable presence eased her discomfort. After passing the security check and proceeding, Shyam notified Candice they were just twenty minutes from their destination—Andrew Gladwell's abode. Offering her a bottle of cold water for comfort, which she gratefully accepted, Candice enjoyed the refreshing drink in contrast to the heat outside.

While driving towards the Gladwell estate, Candice noted Jodhpur's organised roadways and narrow lanes. Although Shyam pointed out historically significant sites, Candice was less focused on his narratives as the anticipation grew. Soon, Shyam indicated their imminent arrival at the domicile.

Candice observed a vast edifice atop a stony elevation, overlooking an artificial lake as they neared, identified by a sign displaying "Desert Vista Resort." The anticipation of what lay beyond the resort's gates, the promise of new experiences and cultural immersion, filled her with nervous excitement. Swiftly, Shyam scurried to assist Candice out of the vehicle, and she stepped onto the dusty ground, ready to embark on this new adventure.

Upon entering the resort's lobby, Candice was captivated by the opulent interior design. Ornate motifs and bold hues decorated the walls while the light fixtures glistened like gemstones suspended overhead. The luxurious ambience of the resort made Candice feel indulged and pampered.

Shyam watched her gaze around in awe. He motioned for her to follow him. "Ms. Candice, please come with me. Let me show you your room."

Shyam led her to a secluded, private hotel part that seemed off-limits to guests. He took her and her suitcase to a large suite with luxurious trappings and a lovely view of a garden. The suite was a sanctuary of comfort, with a plush bed, a spacious living area, and a private balcony that offered a serene view of the resort's lush gardens. The decor was a blend of traditional Rajasthani elements and modern comforts, creating a space that was both opulent and inviting. He gave her thirty minutes to freshen up before they met Andrew Gladwell.

When she rejoined him, Shyam greeted her warmly, and they returned to the main lobby.

"We must now go and pick up Mr. Andrew," he exclaimed excitedly.

"He is visiting a local temple today and has invited you along so you can experience Indian culture."

Candice followed Shyam obediently as they left the hotel, feeling nervous and curious about this new adventure. Shyam expertly navigated the sleek black car through the bustling streets of Jodhpur. As they drove, Candice reached for a guidebook that Shyam had thoughtfully prepared. She skimmed through its pages, soaking in all she could about Rao Jodha, the 15th-century Rajput king who founded their city.

The sun beat down on them as they journeyed through a patchwork quilt of browns, greens, and yellows that spread out before them. Shyam turned onto a road leading farther northward toward Osian.

Candice noticed a massive crowd of people walking along the roadside. She stared out the window at them as they moved methodically along their route. Many in the crowd were singing and chanting in low voices.

"Shyam, what are they doing? Where are they going?" Her voice trembled slightly with fear and confusion.

A gentle smile and reassuring glance accompanied his words. "Ms Candice, these individuals are pilgrims travelling to Baba Ramdev's shrine, situated approximately four hours north of this location," he informed her. With a slight inclination, he suggested she refer to the guidebook. "There may be an informative piece on him in that publication, should you wish to delve deeper."

Candice eagerly flipped through the guidebook, absorbing everything she could find about Baba Ramdev and his shrine as she observed the pilgrims progressing in a rhythmic procession. Baba Ramdev, also known as Ram Devji, was a 14th-century Hindu saint and folk deity in this part of the world. According to legend, he was abandoned at birth and then adopted and raised by a family who taught him the values of harmony and compassion.

He performed many miracles during his lifetime, such as curing diseases, reviving the dead, and blessing barren women with children. At his shrine in Ramdevra, he is worshipped by millions of pilgrims every year.

As Candice read through the guide, she grappled with mixed emotions. Unsure of what to believe, she looked away from the reading material and gazed at the countryside. Looking outside, she saw a continuous stream of people and decided to roll down the window. As the window descended, she was greeted by a chorus of voices from all directions on the street.

The worn, dusty pavement vibrated under the footsteps of the numerous dedicated pilgrims, their expressions showing strong determination as they marched forward together. Candice marvelled at the incredible colourful scene before her - a seemingly endless number of individuals driven by deep-seated belief and purpose. The travellers bore signs of their arduous journey – calloused feet, weathered faces, and sincere eyes brimming with devotion.

Shyam greeted them respectfully, raising his hand in honour before giving a resounding shout in the local language.

The rhythmic pounding of their feet on the hard ground echoed around, shaking the earth and kicking up plumes of dust. Despite the challenging landscape and strenuous exertion, the devotees maintained their

determination; their deep convictions guided them steadfastly on their holy journey.

Surrounded by the crowd of worshippers, Shyam clenched the steering wheel, carefully navigating the car at a measured pace.

The crowd's passionate exaltations blended into a resounding cacophony that drowned out the faint putter of the car's engine.

Candice observed with respect as nimble children darted through the congregation, their palms open, seeking charity.

The fatigue of the journey and a coating of dust could not hide the tranquil certainty etched on the pilgrims' faces. Their sights were set unwaveringly on the distant, gleaming spires of the temple.

Shyam glanced over at Candice, a faint smile touching his weathered features. "For them, the journey is as important as the destination," he said. "Hardship and devotion go hand in hand on the road to enlightenment."

Candice nodded slowly, transfixed by the river of humanity flowing steadily around them. She had never witnessed such raw and unadorned faith, stripped of all pretence. These pilgrims wanted nothing more than to step onto the holy ground and breathe the sanctified air of the temples after weeks or months of tireless walking.

Shyam turned to Candice with an even gaze, his expression unreadable. "They've been walking for days and weeks," he said softly, "to get to a religious place to celebrate the death anniversary of Baba Ramdev, a godman."

The skies above took on an ominous hue, hinting at a deluge that remained withheld. On the horizon, the temple's silhouette stood out against the gloomy skies. Candice struggled to make sense of the spectacle unfolding before her – the deep reverence and unwavering faith demonstrated by those who had travelled great distances to participate in the festivity. What was it about Baba Ramdev that commanded such profound influence over the attendees? Many questions raced through her mind as she stood in awe, feeling small in the face of this sincere demonstration of commitment and unwavering belief. Her usual protective exterior weakened, giving her a rare moment of vulnerability. She returned to reading the guide.

Shyam pointed towards a sizeable grey tower in the distance an hour later. Candice looked up and realised that they had arrived at their destination. The grey building was an immense temple with a vast wall enclosing it. As the crowds thickened, Shyam eased the car in slowly and pulled over onto the shoulder of the road, coming to a stop.

When Candice stepped out, Shyam handed her a scarf and advised, "Please put this around your head, or you might get sunburned. More importantly, it's better if you're not too noticeable – a Westerner walking around with that hair colour will attract too much attention."

She wrapped the scarf around her face, leaving only her eyes, nose, and mouth visible. Shyam gestured for her to proceed to the temple's main entrance, but she hesitated as she saw the crowd.

The deep, resonant sound of drums echoed across the vast courtyard, sending a foreboding shiver through Candice. She and Shyam made their way through the thick crowd, inching towards their goal. Abruptly, Shyam diverted towards a modest wooden door hidden underneath the imposing entryway. Upon his knocking, the door swung open, revealing a woman whose face was obscured by a translucent veil. Engaging in a quiet conversation with Shyam, she offered Candice an unsettling yet intriguing smile. Without any reluctance, this enigmatic figure seized hold of Candice, pulling her briskly into the room before shutting the door forcefully behind them.

Candice felt her pulse quicken as she grappled with their sudden change in direction. The poorly lit hallway seemed to extend endlessly into the darkness. Just as she was about to ask Shyam about it, he gestured for her to be silent and motioned for her to follow him. Candice couldn't shake off her unease as they descended the narrow passageway. The musty smell of old wood and damp stone filled her nostrils as they ventured deeper into the unknown.

As they walked further down, hints of light started to stream in from small holes in the walls. With each one, she looked out, shocked at the chaotic scene of multitudes of people assembling in the courtyard. She was feeling both captivated and scared by what she was seeing. Eventually, without warning, Shyam suddenly stopped. The old woman sat down on a stool near an impressive wooden door. She pinched Candice's cheeks and said something in a language that Candice did not understand.

Shyam burst out laughing. "She wants to know why you're so pale!"

Although Shyam was laughing, Candice was uneasy. After Shyam answered the old woman, she spoke to Candice in a strange dialect. Shyam smiled and explained, "I told her you're English and visiting from another country. She's happy that you're here for the prayers."

They stood at the large wooden door with intricate carvings adorning its surface. Shyam pushed the door open. A wave of warm air hit them as they stepped outside onto a porch opening to the courtyard, which bustled with people.

"Ms. Candice," he said firmly, "please stay close to me. You will not be able to navigate this crowd, and we need to meet Mr. Andrew in time."

Candice silently lowered her head as they moved from the dim corridor into the bright sunlight, momentarily taking them aback. Shyam guided them through the crowd and abruptly stopped, gesturing towards a platform where many people had gathered.

The loud echo of a conch shell resonated across the courtyard, startling Candice into stillness. The sound bounced off the ancient stone walls, trailing into the air. Overwhelmed by the sudden disturbance, she felt the air vibrate with the sounds of a timeless chant sung by hundreds, creating a spectral melody. Shyam quickly seized her wrist and pulled her back, his face marked by a look of grave urgency.

"We won't get any further now," he warned, his voice barely above a whisper as he gestured for her to remain still.

Amidst feelings of bewilderment and obedience, Candice observed that Shyam had settled himself onto the aged temple floor without notice. She was about to critique him for his abrupt decision when she took in her surroundings and noticed all the others seated. Recognising that she was obstructing the view and drawing unnecessary attention, she hesitantly sat on the floor, acutely aware of the curious gazes of the people around her.

"We can't move now," Shyam reminded her gently, waving a comforting hand towards her, "it is tradition."

Feeling exposed and out of place, Candice stood up to find the firmer ground under the watchful eyes of strangers. However, a woman with piercing eyes and a silent command in her movements gestured for Candice to return to her seat, showing equal intrigue and annoyance on her face. At first, Candice resisted, opting to kneel, enduring the unyielding cobblestones against her skin. The increasing pain in her joints eventually convinced her that sitting would be wiser and less painful. With cautious ease, she lowered herself back down and received comforting touches from the group to her head and shoulders—a reassuring welcome into their ritual circle. With a heartfelt smile, she responded, now enveloped in gratitude and respect for this cultural embrace.

The atmosphere was tense as men in pristine white robes and saffron-coloured turbans solemnly entered through an entrance. Their expressions were inscrutable as they moved in perfect harmony, the rustle of their robes adding to the air, heavy with incense. The assembly fell silent as the men placed an intricately detailed wooden chest onto a platform. All eyes were fixed on the chest, filled with anticipation for the unveiling of its contents.

A young priest stepped forward and carefully lifted the lid of the chest. Inside, a sizeable gold dagger with dual blades and an array of elaborate jewellery, including a golden crown adorned with jewels that gleamed in the sunlight, were revealed. The gathered crowd remained hushed, captivated by Candice, feeling unsettled. They turned to Shyam and sensed his intense focus. She clutched at his arm, seeking solace and understanding. "Shyam, what is happening?" she asked quietly.

Overwhelmed with reverence and astonishment, Shyam gestured towards the officiant. "These are the sacred jewels presented yearly to commemorate Baba's sacrifice," he announced, breaking the heavy stillness.

As Candice struggled to process his statement and seek further explanation, two individuals appeared under their dense robes, brandishing shimmering blades, their gazes reflecting malicious purposes. Her pulse quickened, and she understood this event was not a regular ritual. A wave of dread washed over her as it dawned on her that something evil was afoot.

A sudden gunshot shattered the silence, causing panic and chaos within the sacred walls. The crowd scattered, trying to avoid the looming threat. During the chaos, Shyam held Candice tightly, protecting her from the frenzy around them. He remained steadfast, serving as her guardian. As Candice's strength waned, she looked up and saw a troubling scene unfolding on the stage: five men, two holding firearms, had taken over, removed the priest, and boldly laid claim to the valuable treasures before them.

Candice felt her thoughts swirling in chaos as a bizarre scene unfolded. Suddenly, she felt a sharp tug at her side. A girl dressed in traditional Indian garments slipped through the crowd and urgently signalled to her to get out of harm's way. The girl's face was calm amidst the chaos, her complexion glowing against the dirty surroundings, her eyes filled with determined spirit. Despite the young girl's emotional pleas, Candice's sight grew foggy, and the piercing cries in the air seemed to drift away, leaving her in a bewildering stupor.

Candice's gaze pierced through the chaos in front of her; with the determination of a brave warrior, the strange girl sprinted towards the commotion, her skirt fluttering in the wind to reveal agile limbs. Her eyes showed unwavering determination as she confronted the group of five who had stolen the valuable treasure, now carrying a large ornate chest decorated with beautiful brass designs. As they sought their getaway, she procured a humble flick knife hidden within her garment's pleats and aimed it at one of the escaping brigands. What was used for peeling simple fruit with divine luck aided by the deft motion led the blade to spiral in erratic wobbles through the air, embedding it miraculously into the running thief's shoulder. The shock made him miss his step and topple in the dusty complex flow. A rapidly spreading scarlet blotch marred his once-pristine white tunic. The crowd inhaled sharply at this unexpected turn of events, bursting into acclaim for the dauntless damsel who towered unflinching above the prostrate, fuming robber. On the other hand, the dauntless damsel was astonished at her luck and taken aback at the sight of blood from her lucky throw.

The remaining three thieves froze in astonishment, now focused on the bold young girl. Swiftly, one of them brandished a pistol and aimed it at her, his finger twitching on the trigger. But before he could pull the trigger, a bystander lying inert on the ground sprang into action. He seized a handful of sand from the earth and flung it into the shooter's eyes, temporarily blinding him. Seizing the opportunity, he wrested the pistol away and fired a warning shot into the sky, the sound echoing like thunder.

Meanwhile, the remaining men struggling to carry the heavy chest dropped it in confusion upon hearing the shot. The chest landed with a loud thud, sending jewels flying in all directions. In a burst of howls and curses, they attempted to flee but found themselves obstructed by the fierce young girl and the man who now held the gun. With calculated precision, the girl used a short wooden pole she had picked up to deliver vicious blows to two of the bandits, leaving them cursing in pain and clutching their wounds.

The atmosphere shifted as the crowd realised the tide was turning. Fearing the worst, they retreated in a tumultuous uproar toward the raised platform, descending upon the thieves. The enraged mob surrounded the bandits from all sides, launching punches and kicks in unrestrained fury. Even women joined the melee, adding to the commotion with shouts and frenzied scratching at their foes' faces.

Candice crouched on the scorching sandy ground, feeling the sun's relentless heat, making concentrating difficult. Suddenly, police officers emerged to take control of the situation. They dispersed the crowd and arrested the thieves, leaving Candice astonished as her limbs grew heavy.

As the young Indian girl and the man in traditional garb stepped forward, their figures cast long shadows in the blazing sunlight as they approached Candice. The girl's dark hair cascaded down her back as she smiled and reached for Candice's hands. A sensation of disbelief rose within Candice as she gazed up at the pair with a questioning look.

"Hello. I am Sandhya, daughter of Dr Gladwell," she introduced warmly yet formally. Her hand gestured towards the gentlemen nearby, accentuating the title, "Dr. Gladwell." Grinning, the girl added, "Wasn't all that fun?"

Candice's gaze jumped in astonishment as she inspected the gentleman in focus. An amber-hued turban crowned his head, and his feet were adorned with well-trodden leather sandals. His choice of an Indian villager's attire did little to conceal an air of nobility that clung to him. Candice raced to piece together the enigma before her just as the man commenced an unhurried reveal by peeling away the cloth from his crown. What lay before a bewildered Candice was none other than Andrew Gladwell, golden locks cascading down his forehead and the back of his neck.

Caught in a storm of jumbled sentiments, Candice was engulfed in disbelief. The vortex battered her thoughts, and her frame quivered as she knelt on the soft earth, struggling to anchor herself amid the churning tide of the unbelievable reality unravelling around her. Unlike Sandhya's sentiment of fun, Candice felt the opposite of fun.

Chapter 8:

Dr Gladwell and his Daughter Sandhya

"Danger comes in many forms, I suppose. For some, it might be jumping off a bridge or climbing impossible mountains. For others, it could be a tawdry love affair or telling off a mean-looking bus driver because he doesn't like to stop for noisy teenagers. It could be cheating on cards or eating a peanut, even though you're allergic. For me, danger might be getting out from the protective cloak of my family and venturing into the world more of my own, even though I don't know what or who awaits me."

– Dash & Lily's Book of Dares by David Levithan

Candice found it challenging to focus on Sandhya and Andrew Gladwell's silhouettes as they stood before her, and her vision became hazy. She croaked a request for water, to which Sandhya responded by gently allowing some droplets from a chilled bottle of water to flow into Candice's mouth.

"It seems like it's time for us to head back home," Sandhya suggested softly, her voice soothing.

Candice's face formed a faint smile as Shyam Singh took her hand firmly, offering solace. With Dr Gladwell's support, they commenced their slow exit from the lively central courtyard. Nearing the exit, they encountered Commissioner Prabhat Charan, who, with his height and the formality of his police attire, effortlessly commanded respect. He gave a respectful nod before speaking to them in an authoritative and benevolent tone.

"I apologise for the disruption," he said.

Candice felt her heart pound with anxiety as she looked at the five men apprehended and sitting on the ground, surrounded by Commissioner Prabhat's police officers. She was relieved that no harm had occurred to the gathered pilgrims during the chaos.

Commissioner Prabhat and Andrew agreed to return to the Gladwell estate together. The return trip spanned an hour and was marked by Sandhya's lively discourse about the scenic vistas. However, for Candice, Sandhya's ongoing narrative faded into a dull hum as she battled with her mounting anxiety.

Observing Sandhya's captivating visage—with her eyes reminiscent of almonds tinted a soft amber, her unblemished cafe-au-lait complexion and her hair intricately plaited into robust braids—Candice was struck by her natural enthusiasm and ceaseless chatter, which seemed to flow freely like a gentle stream.

A sleek black automobile slid onto the hotel's cobblestone drive, its tyres barely whispering against the stone. Forgoing the pomp of the main entryway, Shyam navigated the car down a more private path to a less conspicuous wing of the establishment. Undeterred by recent events, Candice disembarked with poise, politely declining Shyam's hand. They passed through a lavishly appointed foyer, the walls graced with elaborate frescoes that seemed to breathe life into the space, filled with the intoxicating scent of unfamiliar blooms.

Entering the grand living area, weariness hung like a thick cloak, shed away by their travels. Candice collapsed into the warm embrace of a sumptuous sofa, which seemed to cradle her fatigue.

Dr Gladwell chose an ornate armchair opposite her, and Sandhya's laughter fluttered from her seat at his side, lightening the ambience.

The gravity on Candice's face drew Dr Gladwell's attention, and he smiled and said, "Welcome to Jodhpur." Shyam appeared with a tray of glasses, and Candice eagerly reached for one before turning her attention to Andrew and his daughter, who were still trying to process the day's strange events. "I can't believe what happened today," she said incredulously. "The robbery was insane enough, but seeing you, Dr Gladwell, dressed in traditional clothing and that turban! How did all that come about?"

Dr Gladwell beamed at her. "Having resided in India for twenty years and managed this hotel for ten, I also serve as an important guardian for the

Rathore family of Jodhpur. They've entrusted me with the responsibility to oversee and consult on their substantial philanthropic project—a Museum and Conservatory that celebrates the tribes and cultures of Rajasthan," he explained.

"My wife and I met at a liberal arts college in Virginia, the University of Richmond, in the US. We both studied social science and anthropology there. I was a master's student, and she was a bachelor's student. We fell in love, and I decided to come to India with her to start a new life." He paused to adjust a family portrait on the wall before continuing.

"Her affluent family belonged to the Banjara community. My time in India was initially uncertain, but Sandhya came into our lives shortly after that. Six years ago, following a strenuous fight with cancer, we said goodbye to Pushpa. I remained in India instead of returning to the US. Managing this resort and establishing a significant charitable trust to honour her legacy became my focus. Subsequently, the Rathore family involved me in their project dedicated to preserving Rajasthani culture."

He paused and shifted focus. "The royal family of Rathore, who ruled Jodhpur before India's independence in 1947, were advised by the Bhati family during your visit and informed me about an urgent task you were to address here. They are related by marriage to the Bhati clan. They asked me to make myself available to you and to ensure that you got the necessary support and resources to assist the Bhati family in some matter, which, frankly, no one has shed light on until now. I am hoping you will be kind enough to tell me more."

Candice nodded and then asked Andrew, confused, "I am sorry, the Banjara word you used before. I heard that from Vaibhav Bhati in Johannesburg. They are the nomadic desert tribe of Rajasthan, correct?"

Andrew nodded, his eyes alight with enthusiasm as he elaborated on the subject. "Yes, Banjaras are a type of gypsy originating in this part of the world. They were known for their constant movement and preference for isolation, including keeping their language and customs to themselves. Their history is quite fascinating."

Candice thanked Andrew for his enlightening explanation, her mind buzzing with curiosity and fascination. She wanted to continue the conversation, but the day's events had finally caught up with her, leaving her feeling drained and exhausted.

Andrew misread her gratitude to mean curiosity. He continued with an expansive monologue about the Banjara community.

"The Banjara community of Rajasthan is one of India's most populous and culturally rich nomadic groups. Their lineage harks back to the bygone era of Rajput warriors originating from Central Asia who made their homes in the Thar Desert. Their unique cultural identity is vividly showcased through their vibrant costumes, detailed jewellery, and extensive tattoos. Renowned for their proficiency in livestock rearing, embroidery craft, and traditional music, the Banjaras maintain a robust community bond and adhere faithfully to their age-old customs and legal frameworks."

Andrew noticed his voice waver as he recognised the exhaustion and distant expression in Candice's eyes. Realising the dialogue was largely unilateral, Andrew proposed postponing their business discussion until they met with Commissioner Prabhat Charan the following day. When she seemed to have difficulty remembering him, Andrew explained, "He's the uniformed gentleman, my brother-in-law, and Pushpa's sibling," a revelation that caught Candice off-guard.

Shyam Singh kindly offered to escort Candice to her room and organise dinner. Despite his hospitable welcome, Candice's tiredness was relentless. With gentle persuasion from Andrew, she retired to her quarters to rest.

Following Shyam Singh to her living quarters, Sandhya's conversation about the local climate filled the air as they strolled through the narrow lanes. Later, after a simple yet comforting dinner, Candice retired to her lavishly decorated chamber. The intricate animal embroideries on her soft, inviting bedcover seemed to leap out at her, captivating her attention as she settled in for the night. Soon, she drifted into a restless slumber, entering a vivid dream world. She found herself lost and disoriented in the vast expanse of the Rajasthan Thar Desert in her dream. Desperately seeking water and shelter from the unforgiving environment, she struggled in vain. The intense sun beat down upon her, scorching her parched skin despite the sweat glistening on her body. Every step she took burned her feet through her shoes, and the unending horizon mocked her sense of helplessness. Overwhelmed by fear and isolation, she realised the gravity of her situation — she was entirely lost with no hope of finding her way back. The profound silence of the desert swallowed her pleas for help. At one point, a fleeting illusion of a lush oasis tantalised her, only to vanish as she drew closer. Eventually, she collapsed to the ground, tears flowing as she fought to catch her breath.

As the new day began, Candice awoke with an intense hunger and a sense of being out of place in the unfamiliar surroundings. She tentatively proceeded to the living room, where she encountered Andrew and Commissioner Prabhat, who were deeply involved in an animated conversation. Upon her arrival, they both stood in a gesture of respectful greeting. Andrew gave her a glass of water with a look of restrained anticipation as if he were waiting for her to initiate something.

Andrew gestured for everyone to sit in the comfortable armchairs along the room's side. Candice took a cautious drink from the glass he had provided and settled in a chair, with Commissioner Prabhat quietly taking a spot to her left. Looking up at them, Candice gathered her bravery to begin speaking.

"Thank you for having me here," she began, her voice tinged with urgency. "I'm not sure what the Rathore or Bhati family told you, but I'm here in India on a mission of utmost importance. They urgently want me to uncover a mystery shrouded in secrecy for far too long."

Before she could finish, the door burst open, and Sandhya rushed in. Her sudden appearance added a surprising twist to the unfolding story. Her face was a mix of worry and urgency as she hurried over to Candice.

"How are you feeling, Candice?" Sandhya asked anxiously.

But before Candice could answer, Andrew cut in quickly, his interruption shifting the focus of the conversation.

"Why don't you just tell us what happened, and we can determine whether it's the beginning or end of your story?" he suggested calmly.

Candice could not help but smile reservedly when she saw the sixteen-year-old girl by her side. "I'm glad to see you up and about! You are quite resilient, it seems. After the temple chaos, it's great to see you now carefree and relaxed."

Sandhya nodded eagerly and tugged at Candice's arm. "We must have breakfast before you start a conversation with Dad and Uncle Prabhat," she said urgently.

Candice glanced at Andrew, who had also risen to his feet. "Forgive my rudeness," Andrew said with a sheepish grin. "We must eat first before diving into business." He led the way towards the dining room attached to the living room, where a spread of delicious Indian dishes awaited them.

Candice sat at the table, her eyes darting back and forth between Sandhya and Andrew. Her mind raced with a flurry of thoughts, leaving her face contorted with confusion. Sensing something amiss, Andrew turned to her and asked what was wrong. Candice hesitated before finally voicing her question.

"I know why you're in India, and you showed me a photo of your wife, but I can't understand why you dress like a local and act the way you do,"

A small smile played on Andrew's lips as he tried to stifle a laugh at her naive inquiry.

"Is that all that's been bothering you?" he chuckled, standing up from his chair. He gestured towards a portrait hanging on the wall of an Indian woman draped in traditional garb.

He murmured, a tinge of melancholy imbuing his voice, "Pushpa, Sandhya's mother, departed from this world when Sandhya was merely ten years of age. She was my life's greatest treasure and a woman of vibrant passion, pouring her heart into the community. Above all, it was with her by my side that we steered this enchanting hotel."

An uncomfortable silence filled the room until the Commissioner broke it with quiet clinking sounds as he settled his cutlery and dabbed at his lips with a napkin.

"He credited Pushpa with the feat of domesticating that formidable creature," he remarked, gesturing towards Andrew, who responded with an appreciative grin to the allegory. Turning to give Sandhya a gentle tap on the head, he said, "It's an honour to be Pushpa's sibling and the uncle of such a delightful and spirited young one."

When Pushpa's name was mentioned, it seemed to bring a palpable sense of absence, but Sandhya pushed that feeling aside. She enthusiastically described the various Indian dishes before them, using expressive hand gestures to paint a vivid picture. Although the Commissioner and Andrew had mixed emotions, they both looked proud.

Meanwhile, Candice enjoyed the familiar flavours of toast, jam, and boiled eggs, finding comfort in this moment of sensory bliss before her world changed forever.

Despite feeling tempted to try the unfamiliar Indian dishes on the table, she reminded herself to focus on what was comforting and familiar.

Sandhya watched with amusement as Candice missed an unforgettable gourmet experience due

to her reluctance. She eagerly dug into a bowl of hot and spicy vegetable broth, tears springing to her eyes as the fiery sensations burned her tongue. Yet, she continued to eat it all, earning Candice's unspoken admiration.

After breakfast, Andrew led Candice back into the living room and quickly ushered Sandhya out of sight.

"You have a story for us?" Andrew asked, raising an eyebrow at Commissioner Prabhat, his guest. "Let's hear it then."

Candice's voice echoed through the room, her delicate tone carrying the weight of her words. She spoke of her visit with Avinash and Vaibhav Bhati at their lavish Houghton mansion in Johannesburg, carefully revealing the details of their conversation. Andrew listened intently, his sharp eyes searching for clues she missed. The tension in the air thickened, uncertainty hanging heavy in the room.

Finally, Andrew narrowed his gaze and spoke sternly. "I understand what you have told us, but what is this mystery? How can you hope to solve something shrouded in secrecy for three hundred years?"

Candice met his gaze with unwavering determination. She knew she was the only one who could unravel the family's enigma, and the key lay buried in the past. Taking a deep breath, she replied.

"I believe I can do it, Andrew... with your help. Some days back, I was concerned. I felt I was on a goose chase, but I owe it to Avinash Bhati and his family to do my best to solve this mystery before I call it quits."

She paused, her mind racing as she struggled to find the right words.

"It's difficult to explain," she began hesitantly, "but there was an event long ago involving a member of the Bhati family and a gipsy girl. As a result, a curse was placed upon them, causing every male member to suffer from strange illnesses or meet with inexplicable accidents," Candice's voice faltered momentarily before continuing firmly, "My client, Avinash, is just over sixty years of age. Still, he has been bedridden for years due to an unknown sickness."

Candice trailed off as she noticed both men staring at her with rapt attention. Her heart sank as she braced herself for their disbelief.

"I know how implausible this all sounds," she said apologetically, "but the Bhati family desperately needs someone to investigate, and they've entrusted me to come here to India and seek your help."

Andrew and Commissioner leaned in, their faces etched with concentration as Candice spoke. The Commissioner suddenly leaned back in his chair, his sharp eyes narrowing as he mulled over her story.

"Perhaps, before we continue any further," he suggested calmly, "we should all have a glass of brandy. It will add some much-needed flavour to your tale, Miss Candice."

Andrew's face lit up, and he jumped out of his seat. "Brilliant idea! Nothing like a good drink to accompany a good story." Candice was taken aback by the suggestion for brandy so early in the day. She politely declined.

Undeterred, Andrew hopped over to the bar in the corner and poured two glasses with practised ease. He handed one to the Commissioner and took a hearty sip from his glass.

"Now then," he said, turning to Candice with eager anticipation, "let's hear more about this mystery... Oh, by the way, let's not forget that this girl you're talking about is a Banjara!"

Candice felt a hint of nervousness creeping in. She had expected them to dismiss her story as absurd.

"Do you want me to share such a strange tale now, or should I save it for later?" she asked tentatively.

"Of course, you must share your story!" Andrew exclaimed excitedly. "This is India, after all - the land of mystics! Anything is possible here. So, go on, tell us what happened!"

As Candice took a deep breath, the room fell silent in anticipation of her storytelling. Her hands moved gracefully, gesturing with raw emotion as she delved into the forbidden and tragic love that unfolded between a Prince of Rajasthan and a Banjara girl. Andrew and Commissioner sat on the edge of their seats, completely captivated, their eyes widening with fascination as they hung onto her every word. When

Candice revealed that the Banjara girl had cast a curse upon King Balchand's bloodline, a palpable shiver ran down their spines, and they found themselves unable to tear their gaze away from Candice's flushed face.

Candice took a sip from the glass in her hand. Suddenly, she realised that a glass of brandy had been secretly handed her during the conversation. It was a welcome relief and enhanced the atmosphere of the room. The melting block of ice tinkled in her glass, reminding her to continue.

"So far, so good, but what does it have to do with the Bhati family sending you here?" enquired Andrew.

Candice smiled. "Don't you see, the Prince is one of the ancestors of the Bhati clan!"

The Commissioner asked, "So, what if he is their ancestor? Does that mean something?"

Candice's tongue roved over her lips like a restless snake, desperately parched from speaking for so long. The Commissioner and Andrew looked drained as they gulped the overly watered last few drops in their glasses.

Chapter 9:

Where to From Here

"I, who have also been betrayed, assassinated and cast into a tomb, I have emerged from that tomb by the grace of God, and I owe it to God to take my revenge. He has sent me for that purpose. Here I am."

– The Count of Monte Cristo by
Alexandre Dumas

Sandhya broke the silence in the room by entering with a tray of steaming food. She abruptly stopped at the melancholy sight of the three sitting, still and quiet.

Andrew stood up abruptly and addressed Sandhya, "What are you doing here? You'd better go back outside while we finish up this conversation." Sandhya grinned mischievously while replying, "Finish up what? I have been listening to your conversation, sitting still like a mouse in the corner of the room. It's such a gruesome story! Whatever happened to Neelam?"

Candice started to force a smile, but it soon faded into nothingness.

"This is not a bedtime fable, my dear. It's serious business that you should not be involved in."

Sandhya nonchalantly shrugged. "Stories like these are common in India."

The Commissioner fixed an unyielding gaze on Candice and asked, "How did Neelam meet her end?"

Candice sighed heavily and continued weakly. "From what I have heard, she had been sealed off inside some dungeon alcove."

Andrew swallowed and tried to suppress the scepticism in his voice. "She was locked away alive?" His voice shook. "Okay, tell us how we can help you, Candice; what is our part in this?"

Candice smiled faintly. "The truth is, I haven't even figured out my place in this whole thing, but I am looking forward to your assistance."

Andrew cut in, "Help? What kind of help do you need? Please explain."

Candice stared at Andrew, who stared back at her, expecting answers.

"You know much about Rajasthan and its tribes. You have researched the Banjaras and their clans and tribe loyalties. You can help us figure out how to free the Bhati clan from this curse."

The Commissioner and Andrew exchanged uneasy looks; their scepticism hung heavy. The idea of curses being passed down through generations was difficult to swallow, and even if it were true, there was no telling where to begin.

Sandhya, still eating her meal, piped up. "What is so hard about it? Why not go to the Banjara priesthood at the temple where Mom and Dad married? I am sure Baba Kanmal would know what to do. Neelam was a Banjara girl, wasn't she?"

Candice appeared confused and questioned, "I am sorry; what do you mean by where your parents got married? What does that have to do with anything? Also, who is Baba Kanmal?"

Andrew was about to scold Sandhya for her suggestion, but the Commissioner's firm hand on his shoulder deterred him. The Commissioner addressed Candice's query.

"Sandhya is right. My family comes from the Banjara lineage, a group of wanderers with unique traditions and beliefs. When Andrew and Pushpa decided to get married, they honoured Pushpa's heritage by having Baba Kanmal, the respected chief of the Banjara faith, conduct their marriage rituals in the important Banjara Hall of Divinity and Knowledge. This hall is significant to the Banjara people, as it serves as a place to honour their ancestors and divine entities. Baba Kanmal, who is highly respected and wise, might be able to shed light on the mystery of Neelam and Bhanwar and explain any unfortunate events that may complicate things. It seems like a good idea for us to go there."

Candice slowly nodded before asking her next question. "Okay then, when can we meet this Baba?"

Andrew seemed uneasy about this development and replied cautiously. "I do not see any harm in meeting this Baba, but all this seems far too abstract. If this turns out to be a wild goose chase, then I think it would be best that Candice returns to Johannesburg and informs her client accordingly."

Candice's voice grew loud and strained as she repeated, "When can we meet this Baba?"

Andrew replied carefully, "We must leave early in the morning. Baba's temple compound is three hours from here in Ramdevra, but he will be preoccupied with the ongoing Baba Ramdev festival."

Candice's brow furrowed as confusion clouded her face.

"Wait, how many Babas are there? I am sure I heard of this Baba Ramdev and saw a massive procession of people marching towards a shrine."

The Commissioner nodded gravely. "Yes, you saw the crowds of people lined up on either side of the road heading toward Baba Ramdev's shrine in Ramdevra. Although he has been dead for more than four centuries, he still holds immense respect in this part of the world. The crowds are a testament to the enduring reverence for Baba Ramdev!"

"Dead for four centuries! And people still go there? No, flock there!" Candice questioned in disbelief.

Andrew offered a gentle smile and replied in a friendly manner, "Certainly. Why not? I also make it a point to attend a small church around here every Sunday when possible. It has over two thousand years' worth of history. Isn't that so?" Without waiting to answer his rhetorical query, he continued enthusiastically, "When did you last visit a church, Candice?"

Candice rose abruptly and smoothed her skirt before replying flatly, yet with an undercurrent of bitterness lacing her words. "I don't believe in God."

Andrew and the Commissioner stared at each other questioningly but held their tongues. She continued her voice now an icy whisper.

"Anyway, I think a walk would do me good. Plus, I want to do a bit of shopping. Would you like to join me, Sandhya?"

Sandhya shot up from her seat, squealing in delight and ran outside, screaming, "Shyam Chacha! Shyam Chacha! Candice and I will take a ride!"

Candice glanced at Sandhya and asked, "What does Chacha mean?"

"Oh, it means uncle. Shyam Chacha has been with us for years, and my mother treated him like family. He will do anything for me," Sandhya said proudly.

The two bade goodbye to Andrew and the inspector and walked outdoors. The sun was high. Shyam drove up in his car, and they climbed inside.

"Where to?" asked Shyam as he keyed the engine on.

"Ghantaghar," answered Sandhya.

As the car began to move, Candice looked at Sandhya and asked, "So, where are we headed?"

Sandhya smiled and replied, "We are heading to the clock tower or Ghantaghar. It is an old tower with a big clock mounted on it. Like Jodhpur's own Big Ben, although smaller, of course. We can wander around and grab traditional local food if you like. What do you think?"

Candice was not sure. The thought of local cuisine made her anxious, as she had been advised to stick to bottled water and meals from the safety of a kitchen in India. Yet, Sandhya's hopeful gaze nudged her into a reluctant, wooden agreement. "Sure, sounds like an adventure. Let's go."

Wandering around the bustling vicinity of the clock tower for thirty minutes, Candice felt herself buoyed by Sandhya's unbounded zeal as they meandered between vendors with their colourful wares. At a sudden turn, Sandhya's attention was catapulted towards a shimmering reflection. They spotted a quaint shop brimming with glass-encased jewels that radiated amidst gemstones and metals, which captivated their lustre.

"Wow, check this out!" Sandhya cried out, tugging at Candice's sleeve to draw her closer. Candice, seized by curiosity, followed. Upon arrival, they were met with the jeweller's warm reception.

Sandhya surveyed the shining treasures before her, from glittering silver necklaces dotted with sparkling crystals to opulent golden cuffs laden with gemstones. However, a pendant truly enchanted her – a heart-stealing white gold locket bejewelled with diamonds that danced with the light.

"It's beautiful," Sandhya murmured, treating it with delicacy. She faced Candice, her eyes shining, and declared, "You must take this! It would look remarkable on you."

Candice hesitated, considering the enticing locket. Although inclined to refuse and retreat, she succumbed to Sandhya's persuasive enthusiasm. She quickly unveiled her modest necklace, persuading the eager youngster to move on from the temptations of the sparkling shop. Candice valued simplicity much more than the splendour before them.

Suddenly, a frustrated yell of annoyance rang out. It was Sandhya. She was holding onto the lapel of a young man and screaming in anger incomprehensibly. Candice rushed to Sandhya's aid, her heart pounding with fear.

"What happened? What is going on here?"

Her voice barely registered against the commotion, but her presence was enough to draw attention from those in tow. However, Sandhya had fire in her eyes.

Candice hesitated, shocked at the unbridled fury in Sandhya's eyes.

Sandhya had taken off her slipper and was striking the young man on his torso and head with quick, light movements. Her intention was not to harm but to humiliate. The young man pleaded for mercy, but Sandhya continued without stopping. Her improvised weapon rushed, with each strike accompanied by a deep growl of pure rage from her lips.

The scene was chaotic, with the crowd's emotional voices merging into a tumultuous cacophony. Some among them exuberantly cheered Sandhya on, finding joy in the unfolding violence. Meanwhile, others were hurling curses and insults at the cowering man who had resigned himself to the futility of defending against the relentless onslaught. He lay there, arms weakly shielding his head, emitting soft whimpers with each ensuing blow.

Candice felt her stomach churn. She wanted to look away, to close her eyes and pretend this was all just some terrible nightmare. She couldn't bear to watch any longer; she feared that if this didn't stop soon, the young man would be thrashed until something broke in his skinny body.

"Stop!" she cried out, her voice cracking with emotion. "Please, please stop this!"

However, her appeals were ignored by the exuberant shouts of the onlookers. Sandhya raised her slipper high, prepared to strike with decisive force. There was a brief pause when time seemed to halt, as if in anticipation. With a swift motion, she swung the slipper down, and the uproar resumed. The young man now found himself at the centre of a vibrant crowd, voicing their aggressive demands for retribution, even though they weren't directly affected. His shirt had been ripped away, and his raised hands, signalling surrender, failed to diminish their anger. Sandhya struck once more, driven by unchecked anger.

Candice grabbed her hand to stop her. Sandhya looked at her angrily and snarled, "Don't hold me back. He deserves a hiding. He rubbed me on my behind and pinched me hard! Would you hold me back if he did that to you or your daughter?"

Sandhya's words hit Candice with unintended force. Candice recoiled at the thought of what would have happened if it had been her daughter instead of Sandhya.

Candice was astonished when she saw two people dressed in dark clothes with beaded crowns. She pushed through the crowd, demanding an apology from the young man. Standing behind Sandhya was another woman, offering reassurance with her presence and a comforting hand on the young one's shoulder, warding off potential threats. Despite the man's attempts to apologise, his words were drowned out by panicked cries until the enigmatic woman forcefully nudged him away, signalling for him to leave. He left looking defeated yet relieved, like a hunter who denied his prey but escaped a dangerous situation.

As the commotion settled, the disappointed crowd dispersed, no longer part of the action or witness to any form of instant justice. The excitement was over, and their interest had waned to insignificance.

Sandhya regained her composure, and Candice gasped as the two Banjara women took them both by hand. They led them down a small alley and stopped abruptly in front of an old, run-down house. Two chairs stood before it, and the Banjara women motioned them to take a seat. Candice was about to suggest they turn back when she saw Shyam standing behind them silently, watching without saying a word.

Candice questioned softly. "Sandhya, Shyam, do you know these women?"

The two strangers sat on the ground before them, exchanging words in a soft murmur. With a warm grin, Sandhya introduced Candice to the two matriarchs from her maternal lineage, weaving the story of Candice's purpose for being there with playful asides.

Candice's mind was cast back to that tumultuous day at the marketplace when Sandhya's sandals had flown to defend her dignity. The burning question lingered: How far would you go to protect your own? In a whispered snarl, Candice growled, "I'd end anyone who laid a finger on my child."

Wreathed in melancholy, engulfed in these stormy reflections, Candice barely noticed the focused gaze of the Banjara women until she mustered a brittle smile their way. Her hand shook like autumn leaves until it was enveloped by the Banjara matron, who caressed it into calmness, dissolving Candice's fears in her soothing grasp. The elder spoke words woven with warmth, which Sandhya tenderly translated. "Their haven is now yours too."

The old woman told the story without interruption until she handed Candice an item. It was Candice's locket! Candice immediately reached for her neck, realising that her valued locket was missing. She only then realised that it had been missing. The older woman explained the situation; a pickpocket had taken advantage of the confusion to steal the locket during the commotion. He had taken advantage of Sandhya's distraction. However, the observant elderly ladies noticed his actions and skilfully retrieved the locket during the chaos, saving what was valuable. The old woman opened the locket and looked at two photos inside, one of a man and the other of a young girl. Candice took the locket and put it in her pocket. She was nervous about the turn of events and upset about the invasion of her privacy.

Sandhya was chatting with the old woman when she suddenly paused and nervously asked Candice, "They are asking, how did your daughter die?"

Astonishment washed over Candice, her thoughts a whirlwind of bewilderment as strangers unravelled secrets she hadn't uttered to a soul on this journey. Finding her stance, an amalgam of stupor and resolve etched across her features, she prepared to voice her feelings. However, Shyam intervened, his demeanour tranquil, as he ushered Sandhya and Candice towards the car. As they took their leave, the Banjara elder's narrative, rich with enigma, continued unabated. With hesitant steps, Sandhya bridged the language gap to explain to the respected women the true purpose of Candice's visit to Jodhpur. The women suddenly realised instantly, and a sense of calm came over them. They turned to Candice and silently raised their hands in a blessing that spoke volumes in its quietness.

Sandhya said, "They are expressing good wishes for your future efforts as you seek to correct an injustice done to a daughter from their community. Their people have suffered an insult, and you must make sure that the consequences of destroying an innocent love are addressed."

The weight of these words overwhelmed Candice with a range of emotions. She felt surprised and unsure about the future and how this new information might impact her mission. Experiencing a mixture of dread and determination, she returned with Shyam. Her thoughts were in chaos as she contemplated how the old woman could have known about the connection between the image in her daughter's locket and her sorrow.

Candice was suddenly overwhelmed by feelings of frustration and doubt. How did the truth about her daughter's death become known? And how did they learn of the locket with her daughter's photo? She thought she had kept it hidden from Sandhya. Holding tight to the locket in her pocket as if to protect it from outsiders was an instinctive but ineffective reaction.

Candice was filled with mixed emotions, battling remorse and sorrow alongside a thread of optimism. She wondered if her actions were justified and if they honoured her daughter's legacy. She had travelled to Jodhpur to seek justice for two lovers whose lives were cut short by a ruthless monarch. Overwhelmed with uncertainty about what to anticipate or feel, she conflicted between curiosity, apprehension, hope, and desolation.

An oppressive silence marked the drive back to the Gladwell residence. Finally, Sandhya broke it. "They also wanted to tell you your actions will make your daughter happy. It was God's work."

Candice looked out of the window, her expression distant and flat. With a tinge of admonishment, she replied, "Sandhya, let us not talk about my daughter."

Sandhya was oblivious to Candice's caution and persisted despite this being personal to Candice. "Ah, so you have a daughter! I'm curious to know what happened to her. How old would she be if she were here today? I bet she would have had a blast joining us today. Can you share some stories about her?"

Sandhya knew she had made an error as these words left her lips. Candice had tears welling in her eyes. She bowed her head in sadness and shifted awkwardly, looking outside the car aimlessly.

Shyam observed everything through his rear-view mirror with concern and disapproval. In silence, he conveyed his dissatisfaction in Hindi to Sandhya. Without a word, Sandhya quickly moved from the backseat and took her place next to Shyam in the front. This left Candice alone in the back, giving her time to gather for the rest of the journey home. When they returned to the hotel, Candice exited the vehicle with faint tear stains on her cheeks, a poignant reminder of the emotional turmoil she had experienced at Ghantaghar.

That evening, Candice was restless in her bed—sleep eluded her. Memory after memory of her daughter kept her awake. Seeking respite, she closed her eyes and suddenly found herself dreaming vividly. She sat in a wooden chair in the warmth of a snug room, a fire gently crackling. The familiar weight on her lap caused her to look down—her daughter gazed at her with brilliant blue eyes, looking much younger than at her time of passing, with blonde hair being woven into pigtails.

"Mommy, I miss you so much," her daughter said, clinging to Candice's neck. "I wish we could always be together."

Candice replied tenderly, "And I you, my dear angel. You'll forever reside in my heart, no matter the distance."

Her daughter inquired with innocent curiosity, "Where are you, Mommy? Why does it feel like you're so far?"

"I find myself in India, sweetheart—a country rich with beauty, diversity, and culture. Here, I seek knowledge and lend a helping hand to serve," Candice explained.

Her eager eyes looked up at her. "May I see it, Mommy? Will you show me India?"

Candice answered her daughter's request with a smile, guiding her towards the window, unveiling the night sky. As they gazed upon the moon, Candice shared insights about its importance in Hindu culture as a deity overseeing emotions.

The girl, filled with wonder, asked if Candice prayed to this lunar god.

"No, I don't pray, but in times of seeking, I sometimes wish for answers, for an explanation as to why we're apart. Answers never come, yet gods are revered for their might and wisdom in this land," Candice mused thoughtfully.

Her daughter's excitement grew, "It's fascinating, Mommy. Could we ever meet God?"

Holding her daughter closely, Candice whispered repeatedly, "I love you," to which her daughter responded in kind. Time stood still; both mother and daughter embraced, immersed in profound peace, connection, and vitality, even though one was absent and gone forever.

Chapter 10:

Visit to the Banjara Temple

"When every hope is gone, 'when helpers fail, and comforts flee,' I find that help arrives somehow, from I know not where. Supplication, worship, and prayer are no superstitions; they are acts more real than eating, drinking, sitting, or walking. It is no exaggeration to say that they alone are real; all else is unreal."

– The Story of My Experiments with Truth by Mahatma Gandhi

At the break of dawn, as the Gladwell estate stirred to life, deep purple hues gave way to a blazing tapestry of orange across the horizon. An air of silent anticipation hung heavy, punctuated by muted exchanges that mirrored the gravity of the day's onset. Resolute in her decision, Sandhya chose activity over solitude during her school recess, bringing unwitting comfort to Candice with her vibrant banter and youthful zest, piercing the sombre veil that enshrouded them.

While confidently steering through the lively crowds of Ghantaghar, Andrew observed the severe expressions of the others, which added to the solemn atmosphere in the car. He noticed Candice's uncharacteristic silence, especially after the chaos of the market. Her usually sparkling eyes seemed dimmed, and her posture slumped, indicating her inner exhaustion. Understanding her silent struggle, Andrew tried to lift the heavy mood by sharing Sandhya's animated tales of the courageous Banjara women and their fight against oppression, which brought a glimmer of delight to Candice's eyes. Despite her efforts to remain composed, her true feelings shone through like muted sunlight piercing through dark clouds as she hesitantly recounted their adventures amidst the chaos of the marketplace.

"That was a scary event, but I think after his punishment, he won't even consider looking at another girl again," said Candice cautiously. Sandhya applauded, pleased with Candice's approval of her actions.

"We locals navigate legal boundaries through instant justice – it's a method of establishing order," said Sandhya.

While Andrew felt inclined to concur due to fatherly impulses, he apologised for the Ghantaghar occurrence, not wanting Candice to judge India's charm based on that episode.

Noticing the shift in mood, Sandhya quickly steered their talk towards a series of whimsical observations on various unconnected subjects. She casually brought up whatever playful thoughts she had. When they pulled over at a local diner, the proprietor enthusiastically greeted them, and Commissioner Prabhat was welcomed with open arms.

Commissioner Prabhat then introduced Pranay to Candice. "Candice, meet Pranay, my younger brother. He's taken some time off his job to assist you and Andrew on your journey. Pranay has a knack for navigating the streets, which will be an asset to our mission." I reached out to him earlier and requested his help because he has excellent connections within the community and can be helpful."

Candice paid close attention while Pranay, the leader of a branch of the Banjara tribe, took part in the dialogue. "My family has owned this dining establishment for around fifty years. Once the national highway was constructed, our restaurant gained fame and brought us prosperity," he explained.

He beamed with pride as he added, "We now operate four restaurants along this highway, and I have expanded into international export of Indian art to enthusiasts across the globe."

Glancing at Candice, he continued, "But I do not think you are here for the art; my brother Prabhat told me why you're here. To bring two lovers together and break some curse?"

Candice remained silent while Andrew gestured to an empty chair for her, which she took with appreciation. Opposite her, Pranay settled himself and spoke with a steady voice. "It must be obvious now," he claimed, undisturbed by the weight of his revelation.

"Prabhat, my brother, the Commissioner, filled me in about your escapade in India, putting me onto the fact that making those star-crossed lovers meet again was key to breaking the curse." Addressing everyone gathered, he elaborated.

"The crux of our challenge appears to lie with Candice's scepticism regarding the curse. Let us, just for a moment, entertain its existence," he implored, eyes pleading with Candice for even the slightest sign of acknowledgement. When no such recognition came, he pressed on, "Assuming that the root of the curse is tied to the separation of these two souls, our course is clear—seek their reunion. In their coming together, we might unbind this twisted spell."

Pranay reclined with a self-assured grin, pleased by his reduction of complexities. Rattled by his deduction, Candice defensively crossed her arms and cast a sceptical glance.

"Reunite? What is that supposed to mean here? Bhanwar and Neelam have long departed, haven't they?" she scoffed.

Amidst the feast on the table, Sandhya chimed in with cheeks stuffed with delicacies. "Absolutely," she agreed emphatically, as crumbs flew, revealing the apparent truth she saw but which remained a revelation to Candice. "Connecting those star-crossed souls anew is the key; it's how we'll shatter the curse."

As her tolerance waned, a crimson tide crested on Candice's brow. Recognising Sandhya, she clamped down on the irritation that bubbled up with every oversimplified dialogue and ventured an inquisitive probe for clarity. "How do you propose we reconcile two departed lovers? They've ceased to be among the living and returned to the earth. What are you envisioning here? Do you mean to say their spirits should find union once more, or are you alluding to something more mystical?"

Aware that no response would quell her scepticism, Candice reached for a tantalising cluster of dumplings emitting welcoming warmth.

Her vexation lingered like an undercurrent while bewilderment spun her thoughts like leaves in the wind. Yet, as Commissioner Prabhat's ebullient reply came forth, it was evident that Candice's sceptical remarks had inadvertently inspired enthusiasm.

"Precisely, Candice! Souls are immortal. Merely, the flesh is fleeting. We could converse with the clerics at the Banjara shrine and arrange everything. Those souls must intertwine beyond time."

Listening to this passionate proclamation, Candice pondered the depth of Hindu beliefs about the soul entrenched within the Indian consciousness. She considered the Hindu perspective of the soul as everlasting, unbreakable, and separate from the physical form. This belief system holds that the soul traverses through multiple rebirths until it achieves moksha—the ultimate state of liberation and the raison d'être. Candice speculated whether the sweethearts Bhanwar and Neelam had ascended to heaven or were adrift in limbo, a purgatory, yearning for each other's presence.

While the other participants encircling the expansive table concurred and partook of the spread, Candice sensed her bemusement morphing into dismay and resentment. Nonetheless, she managed to hold her sentiments at bay. In reflection, she embraced the endemic Indian stance of fatalism, nonchalantly shrugging and softly echoing, "Together in perpetuity." Seizing another serving of the enticing dumplings, she said, "Quite delectable, indeed."

Not long after that, the entire party hopped onto the minibus under the capable wheel of Pranay, who had woven himself into the local fabric better than most strangers. En route to see Baba Kanmal, Pranay unwrapped stories of the temple, the Banjara folks, and their storied pasts. But Candice picked up on a subtle disquiet in Pranay's thorough narrative, a tension borne perhaps from missing threads in their shared tapestry of cultural insights.

Slick with sweat, Pranay steered towards the timeworn Banjara shrine, leaving the driver-side window down against the whole zeal of the air conditioning, trying to cool even as a sweltering breeze wafted through the compartment. Sandhya's fingers danced over a map that Pranay had extracted from the glove box. She cautiously unfolded it, inadvertently ripping a corner when some stubborn part gave in. The map depicted Rajasthan's contours.

As Sandhya's fingertip navigated the ornate pathways etched on the map, Pranay pointed out a region, his passion bleeding into a rich account of its profound importance to the Banjara clan. He painted a picture of a hallowed juncture where couples would congregate to honour their lineage deity, the Kuldevi, upon entering matrimony. Meanwhile, Candice leaned in, curiosity piqued, and drank in Pranay's discourse as he elucidated her latent questions, detailing, "The term 'Kuldevi' is an endearment for a goddess esteemed by our kin—guardians imbued with deep-seated reverence in our collective memory and belief system."

The concept escaped Candice's grasp, so Andrew leaned in with an elucidation. "Imagine it as our own Lady of the Lourdes with a twist. We Catholics view it through one lens, while Hindus gaze through another. I've embraced both, being half Hindu by choice, so I relish both narratives."

Candice retorted dismissively with a tone sharp as a sabre. "It's all the same to me. Gods, divinity, I don't buy any of it! Give me solid facts, not superstitions – an unveiled truth is our only salvation!"

In response, Pranay's eyes bulged wide with mock shock, lacing his words. "How can you dismiss God so readily? To deny a higher power is sheer irreverence! No life can unfold in full without recognising the celestial!" His volume soared, punctuated by an airborne index finger for drama.

"Shunning temples? That's within reason. Are you avoiding marriage? Perhaps understandable. But forsaking belief in God—that crosses the line! Faith and spirituality are pillars of human existence, giving us a compass for purpose, morality and meaning."

As tension mounted, Andrew intervened by placing a steady hand on Pranay's shoulder and speaking tranquilly to him in Hindi. Pranay's fervour dissolved, although his look towards Candice was filled with pity, prompting her to turn her gaze to the solitude of the window.

As the car raced down the sweltering asphalt highway, Candice absorbed the rugged beauty of the desert landscape. Scattered cacti and shrubs dotted the sandy terrain, intertwined with patches of muted greenery. Along the roadside, vibrant houses and eclectic shops paraded various wares and services. She caught glimpses of women draped in vivid saris and men adorned with turbans as they went about their daily routines. Some strolled on foot, while others zipped by on bicycles or motorbikes. She spied children engrossed in whimsical play with kites and balls, their laughter dancing through the air. The stark contrast between this region's uncomplicated yet lively existence captivated her.

Upon their arrival at the temple, Candice and Sandhya were greeted by a thoughtful-looking man in saffron robes adorned with a prominent mark on his forehead.

They observed as he gently marked their foreheads with the same sacred symbol, causing Candice to flinch reflexively. Sensing Candice's unease, Sandhya promptly draped a scarf over her exposed shoulders, adding a touch of reverence to their temple visit. After removing their shoes at the entrance, they proceeded into the main hall, where a gathering of devotees had already assembled. Finding a serene corner, they settled onto luxurious cushions.

As the sun reached its zenith, a priest cloaked in resplendent orange robes entered the temple, enveloping the space with the fragrance of incense and the musical echoes of bells against the ancient stone walls. The air was filled with vibrant chants dedicated to Hindu deities, stirring Candice with an overwhelming exhilaration.

Feeling energised by the atmosphere, Sandhya encouraged Candice to join the choir of voices. Their harmonies blended seamlessly as Candice was swept away by the music and the present moment, savouring the blissful escape. Words failed her, but she started mumbling an old-school prayer without thinking.

After the chants subsided, the crowd surged forward to seek blessings from the priest. Candice navigated through the crowd, caught up in the collective enthusiasm and devotion. Amidst the multitude, she stood as a mere anonymous soul, united in their shared enthusiasm.

Following the priest's blessings, Sandhya led Candice to a more secluded part of the temple.

Andrew and others were conversing with a rotund, short man garbed in saffron robes and a matching turban – Baba Kanmal. Approaching him, Candice couldn't shake the reverence for this seemingly holy figure, emanating spiritual wisdom and warmth.

Baba Kanmal's eyes sparkled as they approached, and he motioned towards a small group of elderly, weathered men seated on the ground, somewhat obscured from view. He addressed Candice directly. "Sister, I am Baba Kanmal, the main priest and leader of the Banjara community. I welcome you here in our humble temple."

Candice could not help but feel surprised when she heard him speaking fluent English. She smiled meekly and formed her hands into a gesture of respect. Her curiosity peaked, and she blurted out, "You seem to speak perfect English!"

Baba Kanmal smiled as he responded, "It is only natural that I should speak English well; I hold a master's degree in theology from Oxford University."

Candice was dumbstruck. She had not bargained on this revelation. Before she could remark, Baba Kanmal elaborated.

"At the tender age of twelve, I renounced the material world with my parents' blessings and delved into a devoted study of Hindu scriptures. My thirst for knowledge led me to explore comparative religion, seeking to understand and apply various philosophies and practices to uplift and empower myself and those around me." His words hung heavy in the air, and his pause was deliberate as he sought to emphasise their importance. Then, his gaze locked with Candice's, he continued. "I am a unique blend of both dogmatic and pragmatic simultaneously. These days, I focus on passing down the knowledge and wisdom acquired through my studies and my love for my community to the younger generation. True transformation lies in sharing what we have learned."

Andrew paid homage to each revered figure as they sat on the floor before conversing.

With Commissioner Prabhat at his side, offering further insights, Candice couldn't help but notice the group's occasional upward glances, apparently seeking divine intervention or guidance during their ongoing discussion.

Taking a seat next to Candice, Sandhya began to translate their speech. "They were discussing your visit and what you are looking for. They seemed astonished to see a foreign woman here trying to solve a conflict from three centuries ago between the Bhati clan and Banjara community."

Candice paid close attention as the discussion intensified. Eventually, the elders stood up and departed, leaving only Baba Kanmal there. He quietly took a rosary from his pocket and ran its beads through his fingers. His tone was calm and precise as he spoke.

He thought momentarily and said, "I believe the Bhati clan should accept their situation and move forward, but it's also important to acknowledge that holding a grudge for over three hundred years might not be productive. Our Banjara ancestors have recorded similar stories in ancient scriptures. The four priests who just left the temple can vaguely recall stories about a ruler who, in grief over his lost son, seized the chief's daughter. However, the clarity of these events has been obscured by time."

Candice sensed the tension in the air as Baba Kanmal appeared about to close the door on them, but then he continued speaking. "The elders are currently discussing with our librarian, Kailash. We have an extensive collection of folklore and legends that have been passed down through the generations. I am familiar with the tale of a Banjara chief who had his fingers severed by a cruel Rajput king. This legend will guide our search," he declared, allowing the words to sink in. With a significant glance, he turned to Candice and Andrew and asked, "Would the two of you be interested in accompanying librarian Kailash on the hunt for these materials? They are stored in an underground chamber right here in the temple."

Candice felt her heart racing when she heard the reference to the storage area. Her eyes widened when Andrew leapt up in excitement with a yelp. Andrew asked excitedly, "Candice is welcome to come, but these documents would be in Hindi or the local dialect, so how can she make sense of them?"

As Baba Kanmal grinned broadly, Candice's eyes sparkled with optimism when he revealed, "You'll find it interesting that we've catalogued everything using English dates, and even the indexing keywords are in English. It could require hours to comprehend it fully, but you can likely connect the dots."

Kanmal motioned for the group to keep moving, and they obediently trailed after him.Sandhya hesitantly brought up the rear. Andrew shot Sandhya a stern look and gestured for her to stay back.

"Sandhya should stay with the rest of the group. She doesn't belong here."

Ignoring her father's warning, Sandhya stepped forward with determination. She fixed Baba Kanmal with a steady gaze and, in a resolute voice, cleared her throat to speak.

"Baba, I have a stronger claim to be down there than anyone else. My father became part of the Banjara clan when he married my mother, but I am my mother's daughter - a true daughter of the Banjara clan. Please consider my request and grant me this opportunity.

Baba's laughter resonated through the temple, startling onlookers. He waved his hand in approval and spoke to Sandhya in a language she didn't recognise, filling her with joy. Kailash flicked on a light switch and led the way, hands folded in reverence, into the depths of the Banjara temple. Andrew, Candice, and Sandhya followed with thick anticipation, struggling to contain their excitement as they descended the winding staircase.

Chapter 11:

My Prince, Where Art Thou

"Their book shall be set before them, and you shall see the sinners dismayed at the inscribed. They shall say, "Woe to us! What can this book mean? It omits nothing, small or great: all are noted down!" they shall find their deeds recorded there. Your Lord will wrong none."

– The Holy Koran, Surah 18, Verse 49

The staircase descended rapidly into the temple's depths like an imposing chasm. They continued their descent, leaving the hall behind. The stairs appeared to shrink, casting eerie shadows from the dim lights mounted along the steep steps, which whispered ancient riddles and mysterious knowledge. This collection of esoteric books and hidden wisdom was as captivating as it was unsettling, veiled by the heavy cloak of bygone eras.

The knot of apprehension in Candice's throat tightened as she followed her group. The scant glow from timeworn oil lamps failed to chase away the creeping sense of fear engulfing them. With a tremor in her voice, Sandhya muttered under her breath, "Where does one even start?"

Their guide, the librarian Kanmal, motioned them towards a grand table where he revealed a vast pristine chart paper. He began his questioning with such exactness in a subdued murmur that contributed to the already strained ambience of the chamber. As Andrew shared insights upon each inquiry, the information flowed through Sandhya to an eager yet nervous Candice. Suspense saturated the air, with every soul perched on tenterhooks, longing to strip away the enigmatic veil masking the truths sprawled out on the chart.

"What was the name of the Rajput king?" the librarian asked.

"Balchand Bhati," Andrew replied. "And his wife's name was Vanshikha."

"And which city did he rule over?"

"One or more of the principalities around Jodhpur," Andrew answered.

Delighted with the valuable information he had gathered, the librarian began searching through the library's extensive collection for a specific treasure. After navigating the endless rows of books, he finally discovered a tattered goatskin scroll with Hindi script written in antique ink. Carefully, he unfurled the scroll on the reading table for closer examination while Sandhya looked on, curious about what he had found. As she followed the ancient words with her fingertip, a puzzled expression formed on her face, and her voice brought the words to life in the peaceful space.

"Rao Jodha founded Jodhpur in Vikram Samvat in 1516," Sandhya recited, confused. "That would make it the 14th century since Vikram Samvat is ahead of the Western calendar by..."

Andrew interjected to complete her sentence, "57 years. So, 1516 would mean 1459 AD."

The realisation dawned on them all—they had stumbled upon a piece of history much older than they could have ever imagined. The thrill of this discovery sent a shiver down their spines, igniting a spark of excitement in the room.

Candice wanted to know more about this calendar notation, but the mustiness of the room was getting to her, and she hesitated to open her mouth and breathe in something unknown or unwelcome.

Andrew quickly explained that Candice was waiting for clarification on the calendar references.

"That is the Hindu calendar. It is off by about 57 years from the Gregorian calendar. Ahead, that is!"

With intense focus, Sandhya quickly untied the complicated knots that held the numerous parchments and scrolls together. Each strip of aged paper revealed another clue, slowly uncovering the intricate ancestral web of Rao Jodha and his family. As she unfurled each scroll, her heart raced faster, a mix of anticipation and suspense filling the air.

Taking over where Sandhya left off, Andrew's eyes scanned the ancient scripts adorned with ageing gold on the fragile parchment. Now covered in dust, his finger followed the family connections, navigating the complex lineage of Jodhpur's nobility. His eyes locked onto an unexpected detail, sending a surge of excitement through his body. Filled with genuine enthusiasm, he jumped to his feet, tapping eagerly and rhythmically against the leather as a revelation dawned.

The librarian's eyes bulged with astonishment at Andrew's sudden outburst. Once his composure returned, Andrew recounted, "Back in the 17th century, Mandore fell under the reign of King Balchand Bhati. The archives reveal his marriage to Vanshikha of Osian and their three offspring, with Bhanwar among them, only to be branded as 'cast aside post-mortem' in historical scrolls."

A chill ran through Candice as she pondered the grim notion of a tribe renouncing their own after death. She murmured incredulously, "How could such a thing even occur?" With a solemn nod, Andrew confirmed her trepidation. "Typically, it's when someone brings shame or dishonour upon their kin," he clarified, arching an eyebrow and locking gazes with Candice. "Such as tying the knot with a girl from the Banjara community."

As Sandhya and Andrew locked eyes, they silently acknowledged the weight of this discovery. Andrew proceeded to piece together the puzzle, showcasing its pertinence to their quest for the fabled Prince. "Now we're certain the Prince was more than a mere fable," he declared, briskly rubbing in anticipation.

Candice was still sceptical, as they were not going after the Banjara woman or her leader but Balchand and his descendants. Meanwhile, Sandhya was having a lively conversation with the librarian, and both burst into loud laughter, which only heightened Candice's curiosity even more. In the background, the librarian was fervently searching through ancient documents, muttering cryptic words only he seemed to understand. Candice felt increasingly uneasy with each translation from Sandhya, uncovering yet another layer of mystery.

"It would be virtually impossible to find a Banjara chief and his daughter without an approximate year and a location close to Mandore or Jodhpur," she said.

Candice was initially confused but understood that tracing the well-documented Rajput lineage could help find the Banjara chief. The librarian instructed Sandhya and Andrew to search different sections of the walls covered in Hindi numerals. Andrew told Candice the answer was somewhere between his and Sandhya's shelves. However, Candice was frustrated by the barriers of shelves filled with scrolls and books between Sandhya and Andrew. She prepared herself for a tedious task. Andrew searched through the records and cited references out loud, but he failed to find the information, as the librarian repeatedly disagreed with his findings.

An hour into examining countless unrelated documents, Sandhya stopped to have the librarian look at a painting she found. It depicted two young people pulled apart by threatening hands. The painting had a dagger and inscribed text on the backside. The librarian displayed the painting so Sandhya could recite what was written.

In the desert sands, a tale is spun so bold,

Of a Banjara girl with a heart of untold gold.

She gave her love to one not of her kin,

Defying the strict rules society pinned.

Their whispers echoed 'neath the banyan's breath,

A love so fierce, it knew no fear of death.

Their story, like the peacock's vibrant fold,

In songs and sagas, eternally retold.

Though flesh may fade, in the desert's song, they soar.

For in each note, their spirits dance once more.

It tells of Neelam with her bangles' chime,

And Bhanwar, whose love transcended space and time.

Their love, though pure, met a tragic breath,

Yet, in the end, their souls escaped death.

For stories of their passion will forever be retold,

In songs, where their eternal love unfolds.

Though some may perish, in melody, they thrive,

For death begins a tune, where love survives.

It sings of Neelam and Bhanwar, torn by fate's shove,

A ballad of cursed lovers seeking reunion above.

With her final whisper, she cast a vengeful fuss,

"May those who part us bear a curse, as thus.

Until in the afterlife, our spirits align,

This curse shall linger through the sands of time.

Though the world may forget, the desert sings their lore,

For in its heart, their spirits meet forever.

It sings of Neelam, with hennaed hands so fine,

And Bhanwar, whose love crossed the bounds of time.

With wide eyes filled with excitement, the librarian was wholly absorbed in deciphering the ancient parchment. His fingers traced the intricate markings and symbols as he mumbled calmly, almost as if in a trance. The room's atmosphere seemed to intensify, crackling with electric energy, as the librarian jumped from his seat and made a beeline for a musty old chest nestled in the corner. His hands moved frantically, sending books flying as he searched for something. He triumphantly emerged after what felt like an eternity, clutching a weathered book close to his chest.

Returning to the table, his eyes glittered with curiosity and anticipation as he carefully opened the book as if revealing a long-lost treasure. Sandhya, standing by his side, couldn't contain her amazement. "This is a book of Banjara love stories! It's like a collection of Romeo and Juliet, but for the gipsy community!" she exclaimed, her eyes widening with wonder.

Meanwhile, Andrew trailed closely behind the librarian, unable to conceal his growing anticipation. His gaze was fixated on the unfolding events, stealing glances over his shoulder every few moments. Suddenly, the librarian came to an abrupt halt and pointed excitedly towards a page in the ancient tome, revealing a sepia-stained illustration that sent a shiver down Andrew's spine. He staggered backwards, nearly causing an armchair to topple, his heart racing as he wiped away beads of sweat from his forehead, leaving dirt trails along his cheeks.

Candice joined them, her curiosity piqued. "What have we discovered now? This is taking too long; can we come back tomorrow?" she asked.

Through gritted teeth, Andrew replied, "No, we are almost finished here. This book contains ancient folklore about Bhanwar and Neelam, star-crossed lovers who met their tragic end at Bal Samand Lake near a small village on its banks. Legend has it that the village was abandoned by its people, overcome with grief, who moved to Soor Sagar Hamlet."

Candice stood up, a tinge of excitement in her voice. "That's great news," she said, looking at Sandhya. "Now we know much more. Can we go there and search for answers?"

Andrew shook his head. "And do what? Just knowing the place will not help us find out what happened to her body. We don't even know where to start." He headed towards the exit, continuing, "I think it's time to leave and take this matter to Baba Kanmal for further guidance."

Sandhya moved quickly, stooping down to pick up the scattered notes. Then, she delicately arranged them onto the chart before carefully placing them back on the table. As they ascended the staircase step by step, the wooden stairs released a soft creak under their weight, resonating in the deserted hall enveloped in an eerie silence. No devotees were to be seen, with the fading sun casting long, creeping shadows across the premises. Following the librarian's lead, they returned to the room where they had first met Baba Kanmal.

Inside, the air was heavy with the lingering fragrance of incense as the elders and Baba Kanmal were seated, puffing contentedly on their chillums, the smoke creating intricate patterns in the air. Baba Kanmal beckoned them with a rough, gravelly voice. "Welcome back," he boomed, "tell me, what did you find?"

Andrew began to outline their discoveries while Baba Kanmal's eyes furrowed in thought and his lips pursed contemplatively. After a moment, he sharply jutted his chin out to confer with the other four elders. The animated conversation quickly escalated into an argument with one elder, Brother Rajesh, who sounded extremely agitated and forceful. Once the commotion died down and only three elders remained, Brother Rajesh left the room, visibly unhappy. Baba Kanmal then turned his attention back to Andrew and the others.

"We have a solution," he began, but before he could continue, Andrew interrupted.

"Why is the elder Brother Rajesh not keen to help us? He sounded very agitated and angry. What is going on?"

Baba Kanmal's expression grew sad as he gazed at Andrew and then at Candice with sorrowful eyes before replying.

"Surely you can understand his dilemma," he said gravely, "we are facing a wrong inflicted upon one of our daughters. Brother Rajesh believes we would defile her memory and sacrifice by aiding you in righting this wrong. The Banjara gave a curse, and Rajesh does not believe it should be undone."

He paused momentarily before resuming his rapid counting of rosary beads, carried on forcefully.

"But we know that a long time has passed. We must find a way out of this curse to redeem the Bhati clan and free these two lovers from their centuries-long separation! No matter what it takes, they must unite again and be given a proper burial to lift this curse!"

Baba Kanmal spoke with measured calm and unshakeable logic, his voice carrying the weight of years of experience. But despite his confident words, Candice could not believe what she was hearing. She could not help but interrupt, her voice trembling with disbelief.

"I apologise, but I need to clarify. Are you asking about locating them? Unfortunately, they are no longer here. We are uncertain of their whereabouts. Who has taken whose body and to where? Even if we managed to track that information, would their bodies have been disposed of, and funerals already arranged?"

Kanmal shook his head in gentle disagreement, his piercing gaze fixed on Candice as he explained patiently.

"It seems that the spirits of the deceased cannot find peace because they are being affected by a powerful curse. Neelam seems to be a central figure in this mystery, and her beloved Bhanwar appears to be separated from her. It is suggested that the curse will continue to affect the perpetrators and their descendants. It's possible that unravelling the mystery surrounding their bodies and understanding why they were denied a proper cremation may be the key to setting their souls free."

Baba Kanmal seemed to ponder deeply, pausing momentarily before elaborating further.

"According to Hindu beliefs, the soul is eternal and moves on to the next life based on karma after death. Sometimes, souls may be trapped due to violent deaths, unresolved conflicts, or curses. To help them find peace, performing proper rites and prayers is essential. Neelam and Bhanwar's tragic love story seems to have left them cursed and unable to move on. It is imperative to discover what happened to their bodies and reverse the denial of a proper cremation, to break the curse and free their souls."

Candice's mind reeled at Kanmal's suggestion; she struggled to make sense of corpses, ghosts, and restless souls awaiting their fate in limbo. Standing up from her chair, she bowed politely before Kanmal and said, "I think I've heard enough for today." With heavy confusion, she left the hall, searching for Shyam, with Sandhya trailing behind at her father's insistence.

Baba Kanmal turned to Andrew, his expression solemn and grave. "What do you make of all this?"

Andrew took a moment to consider before responding cautiously, "What would you like me to think?" His mind buzzing with questions and doubts, he knew he needed more time to process the strange events unfolding before him.

Brother Rajesh had returned to the group, his face contorted with pain and anger. He intoned a warning to deliver a dire message.

"This is not a battle you can win! Do not force your will against the gods; if you do so, only ruin and destruction will come to your door. It would be folly to go through with this course of action."

Andrew bristled, ready to retort, but his daughter Sandhya stepped forward, her face flushed with anger.

She spoke out fiercely, defending her father. Her voice was sharp and cutting, like the crack of a whip.

"Sir, please don't talk to my father like he is some bystander or outsider. He is actively and personally involved in this, not for personal gain. We are here because Candice has come asking for help, but you seem on a tangent to that objective."

Before Sandhya could blink, a dark-haired man with piercing eyes materialised out of thin air, his hand snatching her delicate wrist in a vice-like grip. She let out a strangled cry as she felt the strength of his hold sending sharp bolts of pain through her arm. In a split second, he produced a gleaming dagger from the folds of his cloak, its blade glinting ominously in the pale moonlight. With a cruel smirk, he aimed it at Andrew's throat before slowly lowering it towards Sandhya's trembling body, taunting them with his power and control. Panic and rage burned through Andrew's veins as he struggled against the stranger's iron grip, but before he could move, the man vanished into the shadows like a ghost. With an enraged scream, Sandhya hurled anything she could get her hands on at the fleeting figure, but all her efforts proved futile as he disappeared into the darkness. Turning to check on his family, Andrew felt a surge of fear and panic as he realised Brother Rajesh was no longer by their side. His recklessness and defiance had led them into this dangerous encounter with a mysterious assailant who may still be lurking nearby, waiting for an opportunity to strike again. The air was tense, and Andrew knew they were far from safe.

Andrew's heart sank as he carefully surveyed the dimly lit surroundings outside the ancient Banjara temple, desperately seeking any clue about Rajesh's or the enigmatic attacker's whereabouts. Sandhya, overcome with fear, was inconsolable, her body quivering as she tightly grasped Andrew's arm for support. Andrew urgently realised they needed to find safety before the assailant reappeared. Determined, he guided Sandhya and Candice swiftly towards the safety of the waiting minibus.

Andrew pursed his lips. He was bothered by Brother Rajesh and the behaviour of one of Rajesh's henchmen, who dared to wave a dagger at them in public. It was a threat. They needed to leave this place immediately.

Standing outside the minibus, they met up with the Charan brothers, Sandhya's uncles, who talked animatedly while taking deep drags on their cigarettes. Getting nicotine into their bodies after the many hours underground seemed to be top of mind for them. They had missed the entire altercation with Brother Rajesh and the audacious young man making open threats with a knife in public.

Sandhya's uncles, the Charan brothers, listened intently as Andrew recounted the harrowing encounter with the mysterious attacker. Their faces clouded with concern and anger as Andrew described the glint of the dagger and the man's vice-like grip on Sandhya's wrist.

"This is outrageous!" bellowed Commissioner Prabhat, his fists clenching at his sides. "Threatening my niece in broad daylight? Right outside our sacred temple? This cannot stand."

Pranay Charan nodded vigorously; his eyebrows knitted together. "Yes, this scoundrel must be found and taught a lesson. I can gather a team and return to the temple to deal with that goon."

Andrew felt a swell of relief and gratitude towards Sandhya's uncles. Though eccentric and stubborn at times, their protectiveness towards Sandhya was clear.

"Please, we need to get Sandhya and Candice to safety first," urged Andrew. "I fear this villain may still be lurking nearby."

"Of course, of course!" Pranay responded. He turned towards Sandhya and enveloped her in a tight hug. "You will come back with us, my dear. We will keep you safe."

Andrew nodded, comforted by the protective brothers' presence. Sandhya tucked herself under Andrew's arm as they piled into the minibus. Though still shaken, her trembling had eased.

As the minibus drove away from the scene of the attack, Sandhya closed her eyes, her heart still pounding in her chest. She desperately longed to escape the haunting memory of the nightmarish assault. But as she drifted into an uneasy sleep, her mind plunged her into a terrifying nightmare that felt all too real.

In her dream, she found herself back in the grasp of the villain, reliving the horror of the assault in vivid detail. She could feel the chilling touch of his hand on her neck, the sensation of his razor- sharp nails piercing her skin, and the searing pain as venom coursed through her veins. His twisted face, contorted with malice, mocking smile, and dark, menacing eyes, seemed to taunt her even within the depths of her dream.

The memory of his voice, whispering threats and taunts in her ear, echoed through her mind, causing her to jolt awake in a panicked frenzy. As she gasped for air, she found herself clutching Andrew's hand, seeking solace and reassurance in the frightening wake of her nightmare.

Chapter 12:

Chained and Still in Pain

"Good night! good night! As we so oft have said,

Beneath this roof, at midnight, in the days

That is no more, and shall no more return.

Thou hast but taken up thy lamp and gone to bed;

I stay a little longer, as one stays

To cover up the embers, that still burn.

– Henry Wadsworth Longfellow

The drive back home was long. The group's minds were abuzz with the information gathered over a very fruitful and tiring day. There were hushed conversations and the occasional outburst between Candice and Sandhya when they recalled a critical piece of information and its importance. Sandhya was doing much better after her short nap despite the garish nightmare she had endured.

The roads were lined with tall trees, their leaves rustling in the gentle breeze as they passed, but none of the passengers noticed them.

Sandhya glanced at Candice, her words hesitant but filled with urgency.

"Do you remember saying that Neelam was buried alive somewhere?" she asked. "If that's true, then Baba Kanmal was right. The two lovers cannot be reunited, and the Prince's soul will not be freed. Those who commit suicide must go through a painful purification process."

She raised her hands and clapped hard for emphasis before declaring, "We need to find out where she was buried!"

Ever the calm presence, Andrew placed a comforting hand on his daughter's shoulder.

"Let's not get ahead of ourselves," he said calmly. He turned to Shyam, who was driving them all back, but remembering something, he pivoted to Commissioner Prabhat and Pranay.

"Can one of you contact Rawal Nath and let him know we'll be heading to Soor Sagar tomorrow?"

Candice, confused, sought clarity on who Rawal Nath was.

Andrew clarified, "Rawal Nath is the name Baba Kanmal gave us. He is the local clan leader of the Banjara who settled in the Soor Sagar area."

At the same time, Pranay grabbed his phone and began making calls to locate Rawal Nath. Soon enough, he received a call back from him and put it on speaker.

Rawal Nath's voice held a deep sadness as he spoke.

"For three centuries, my family has carried the weight of this tragic story of Neelam," he said. "As descendants of Chief Nagarmal's younger brother, we have never forgotten what happened to the two lovers who were torn apart."

Andrew interrupted Rawal Nath before he could become too nostalgic.

"We need your help in uncovering the truth about what happened to their bodies on that fateful day," he stated plainly. "Baba Kanmal wishes to unite them, but we are unsure if it is even possible."

A sharp, disbelieving snort echoed over the line, piercing the tense air. Rawal Nath's voice dripped with doubt as he processed the news.

"Unite the two bodies?" he exclaimed incredulously. "But there are no two bodies! Our Banjara girl's remains were never found, taken away by the king as a trophy of his victory. We fled with only the Prince's body in retaliation and started anew in Soor Sagar. Come to me tomorrow, and we will gather our people to see how we can assist."

The atmosphere inside the minibus was tense as the passengers settled into their seats. Overwhelmed by the day's events and struggling to piece together the information, Andrew was engulfed by fatigue. He sought comfort from Candice, only to find her asleep. A sense of defeat was evident amongst his travel companions. Andrew attempted to converse with Pranay, who continued to drive loyally and was unresponsive to banter.

Upon arrival at Andrew's residence, the group exited the minibus and dispersed quietly in different directions. Given the late hour, Andrew, concerned for their well-being, planned for Commissioner Prabhat and Pranay to stay overnight, saving them from a nighttime journey. Both brothers, worn out by the day, looked forward to some much-needed rest.

Hand in hand, Sandhya and Candice tread softly back to Candice's sanctuary. With a quiver in her voice, Sandhya confessed her dread of solitude and implored if she might share Candice's company through the night.

Silence lapsed before Candice's face broke into a warm, reassuring smile. "You're welcome to stay, my dear."

Sandhya hurried off to change into something more comfortable while Candice remained in her room, calmly combing her hair. Her mind was uncertain, but she felt somewhat relieved after inviting Sandhya.

Candice nestled into the welcoming embrace of her bed. Side by side, they lay, and despite the day's whirlwind leaving Candice spent, Sandhya stared at the ceiling, unburdened and vigilant. Turning to Candice with curiosity brimming in her eyes, Sandhya inquired, permission granted with a nod, "Could you share your daughter's story with me? What became of her?"

Candice was startled by the sudden question when her daughter's name was mentioned, and a flood of emotions washed over her. A heavy silence filled the air, fraught with sorrow and unspoken memories. Then, Sandhya gently touched Candice's trembling hand, offering a sense of calm amid the emotional storm.

As Sandhya carefully examined each photo, she felt a warmth spreading through her at the sight of the precious family captured in the images. However, an unspoken question lingered in the air, waiting to be addressed.

With tears in her eyes, Candice began to explain, pointing at each photo as she spoke. "That's Jadene, my beloved daughter. She and her father, Chris, were lost in a tragic car accident when she was just ten years old. Jadene would have turned sixteen this year," she said, looking at Sandhya with a mix of sadness and love before continuing, "almost the same age as you."

Candice's voice trembled as she recounted the story of her daughter and her husband. It was a tale woven from love and grief, marked by lingering sadness that time had not managed to erase. Her description of Jadene was filled with an unwavering maternal affection that transcended even the most profound sorrow.

"Jadene was our light, the epitome of joy and innocence," she narrated, her eyes filled with grief. "She inherited her father's adventurous spirit and free nature. They did everything together, exploring and seeking new experiences. On that fateful morning, as they set out on Chris's motorcycle, they were unaware of the tragedy awaiting them."

Pausing to compose herself, she continued, "The crash was sudden and unexpected, like a violent storm. They were travelling on the familiar highway near Johannesburg, but it had become unfamiliar that day."

Her words trailed off. "An out-of-control truck caused the crash—the screech of tyres, shattering glass, and then silence. The impact was devastating; they were thrown onto the road. Chris's life ended there, and after fighting for days, Jadene also left us, leaving me with an aching void."

Sandhya was deeply moved by Candice's loss and felt a wave of compassion for her. "This year would have been Jadene's sixteenth," Candice whispered, a fleeting smile on her lips. "She would have been much like you, Sandhya—full of life and dreams. Her spirit lives on in my memories, her laughter echoing through the depths of our souls."

The room was quiet, save for the soft clock ticking, marking the passage of time, a reminder that life moves forward, even when we carry the weight of the past. In that moment, Sandhya felt a connection to Jadene, a girl she had never met but whose story had touched her deeply, a reminder of the fragility of life and the enduring strength of love.

Candice let out a slight shrug and then carefully put the photos away. "There, now you know. Now, let's try to get some rest."

Sandhya held Candice's hand and spoke in an uncharacteristic, subdued voice, a mumble.

"Candice, sorry for your loss. I would have loved to have met Jadene. We could have been friends," Sandhya paused and added, "She seemed like such a sweet and brave girl. I bet she loved reading and writing, just like me. Maybe we could have shared stories and poems and helped each other with homework. Maybe we could have gone to the park, played on the swings or the library, and browsed the books. Maybe we could have laughed, cried, and supported each other through hard times. She would have been a great friend, Candice. I'm so sorry you lost her."

As Sandhya closed her eyes and drifted off to sleep, she suddenly snapped back to reality. Without skipping a beat, she started talking about how she would have loved to explore Jodhpur with Jadene, wandering the markets and helping her pick out colourful dresses and souvenirs. After a while, Sandhya's eyes closed again, and she finally fell into a peaceful slumber.

Candice gazed at Sandhya's face, a faint smile appearing on her lips as silent tears filled her eyes. For the first time in many years, Candice found comfort in the presence of someone who reminded her so much of her daughter. It felt as if destiny had finally answered her prayers. She tenderly took Sandhya's limp hand and placed it gently on her stomach, a gesture she hadn't made since losing her daughter, Jadene.

Candice felt a surge of affection and gratitude for the young girl who had shown her so much kindness and compassion. Sandhya had the same dark hair, almond eyes, and gentle smile. Candice wondered if this was a sign from the universe, a way of healing her broken heart and filling the void that Jadene's death had left. She took Sandhya's limp hand and gently placed it on her stomach, something that she had not done since losing her daughter. She felt a warm and soothing sensation in her womb, as if Jadene was still with her, growing inside her. She whispered a silent prayer of thanks and closed her eyes, hoping to dream of her daughter. She fell asleep peacefully, unaware of the danger that lurked outside.

Candice woke suddenly to find that her hand had gone numb from being tucked underneath Sandhya's head. She moved Sandhya to the side and turned around. What happened next made every hair on her neck stand. Her eyes drifted over to the open window to let in fresh air, only to see a shadowy figure standing still outside. As cold sweat spread across her forehead, a hand appeared through the window, pushing it wide open slowly. Candice opened her mouth to scream, but no sound came out. Overwhelmed by fear, she attempted to pull herself out of bed, but her legs were frozen. The intruder had thrown something into the room. The unidentified object landed with a soft thud on the tiled floor. Candice attempted to scream, but no sound escaped from her lips. Finally, after what seemed like an eternity, a shrill cry did escape her lungs, which led to the intruder fleeing into the night and Sandhya bolting out of her bed in confusion.

Confused and disoriented, the half-asleep girl slowly looked around the dimly lit room and approached the moonlit window, with Candice trailing close behind. In her hasty attempt to reach the window, Sandhya stumbled over an unseen object on the floor and collided with a nearby chair, causing the side table and night lamp to come crashing down onto the hard stone floor with a loud noise. As Candice rushed to check on Sandhya, her panicked screams for help filled the room.

Andrew, startled by the commotion, burst into the room and hastily switched on the lights. He stood frozen in shock at the distressing scene that unfolded before him. There, in front of him, lay Sandhya, writhing in pain, her groans mingling with the distressing sight of blood slowly seeping from the body of a lifeless cat sprawled nearby.

Andrew examined the feline's lifeless form, confused at how it had ended up in their room. Pivoting to Candice from a crouching position still bent over the dead animal, Andrew questioned Candice.

"Tell me what happened here. What did you see or hear?"

Candice, with an edgy tone, gave him a rundown of events. Andrew's face grew livid as he heard Candice tell him of the terror of seeing someone throw an unknown object through their window, which turned out to be the dead cat.

Andrew summoned Shyam and others who appeared at their door to search the grounds for any sign of the perpetrator. Andrew roared with rage as he saw his beautiful daughter Sandhya writhing in pain on the ground. Fuming, he spat, "Who did this? What kind of person would do this and attack a young girl?" His blood boiling, Andrew knelt and tenderly examined Sandhya's left hand, already swelling and broken. His eyes filled with fire. He rose and declared thunderously, "I will find the culprits. Candice, you stay here. Please help with this mess!"

Candice trembled as she gazed at the dead cat, which lay there lifelessly, its neck cut deep in the form of what seemed like a symbol of a dark warning. She staggered away from the scene in shock. Shyam quickly ran to her side, ordering her not to move. Commissioner Prabhat arrived, and they searched through every nook and cranny of the house. He sat with Candice and interrogated her about what had transpired earlier.

Two hours later, Andrew returned home with a very pale and fragile Sandhya, her arm now encased by a plaster cast. Tenderly, he tucked her into bed before returning to where Commissioner Prabhat was waiting for him. He accepted the glass of brandy offered but said nothing until, finally, Commissioner Prabhat broke the oppressive silence in a soft and reassuring tone.

"Andrew, there was no trace of anyone here. Someone is sending you a message. This could have ended much worse."

Candice's face was filled with disbelief and anger as she hissed back, "Look at the damage they have done. Sandhya has a broken arm, and my room is soaked in the blood of a dead cat!"

Her voice had lowered to a whisper as she remembered the gruesome scene.

Commissioner Prabhat replied, "I never said anything happened, but I think this was someone sending us a warning."

Candice hissed in frustration. "Warning? Warning, about what?"

Commissioner Prabhat was unfazed by Candice's interrogative voice. He replied calmly and logically, "A warning to stop searching for the Banjara girl or trying to figure out what happened here. Does that sound like a reasonable explanation?"

Candice stared at him and Andrew before saying through gritted teeth, "Wait a second... if somebody's trying to scare us away from getting to the truth, there must be something they're hiding."

She paused to steady her voice and then continued shakily. "Forget about them—this is personal now. If they mess with my daughter, er, I meant Andrew's daughter, they mess with us all."

Andrew and the Commissioner noticed her hands trembling as she took shallow, unnatural, short gasps of air.

As they returned to their rooms, Prabhat summoned some police officers to stand guard at Andrew's home area at the hotel. They could not dismiss the fear of another attack.

The next day, the group had planned to rendezvous with Rawal Nath at Soor Sagar. However, opting for additional rest led to their delayed departure. They travelled in Pranay's minibus, which rattled so loudly that it hindered any attempt at normal conversation. The general mood did not lend itself to lively chat, and without the exception of perhaps Sandhya — who remained in Shyam's care due to a broken arm — no one seemed inclined to engage. Their journey proceeded without incident, but as they approached the lake and turned onto a dirt road, a man dressed in white with an orange turban gestured for them to stop, calling out to them. "Greetings. Is this the Pranay and his entourage?"

Pranay rolled down his window and replied in the affirmative. He introduced himself and outlined their mission: finding an answer to the Banjara curse.

Their guide, Rawal Nath, skilfully led the weary travellers to a tranquil clearing nestled off the rugged road, where their travel-worn minibus found its temporary repose. Here, the journey would transition to one by foot, as the path ahead was overlaid with a glistening film of moist earth following a night of drenching rainfall.

As they set forth, a minor assembly of curious onlookers congregated, their presence signalled by the occasional spray of earth kicked up from beneath their footsteps. Prickly shrubs flanked the route. Local dogs paused momentarily, their curiosity piqued by the passing parade, before nonchalantly continuing.

Faint strains of music from a distant radio and the tantalising aroma of spices and sizzling oil emanating from the open windows of mud-brick abodes teased the travellers' senses as they traversed the path. Brimming with curiosity and joy, children frolicked beside them while brightly attired women bestowed warm smiles and nods upon the foreigners. Turbaned men paused their labours to offer Rawal Nath a cordial greeting and a brief exchange of words.

Approaching the hamlet's outskirts, the travellers caught sight of a picturesque congregation of villagers gathered outside one of the larger residences. Rawal Nath escorted them into his family's modest dwelling, where his mother and grandmother, a venerable centenarian renowned for her sagacious counsel, resided.

Seating options within the abode varied, from unembellished plastic chairs to adaptable wooden cots repurposed as makeshift benches. A contemplative hush descended over the room as attendants respectfully guided the revered elder to her designated place before the assembled company. Adorned in time-honoured garb and bedecked with shimmering silver trinkets adorning her visage, wrists, and ankles, the matriarch exuded an air of fragile antiquity. Her head was covered, but a cascade of thinning silver was visible.

Despite the etched lines that adorned her countenance, her eyes sparkled with a vibrancy that defied the mark of time. Upon noting the radiant hue of Candice's hair, she tenderly reached out, eliciting joyous laughter from those present.

Turning to Andrew with a knowing glance, Rawal Nath intimated, "You seek answers regarding the fabled Neelam Banjara legend and curse. Gavri Bai holds the key to the knowledge you seek."

Standing before Gavri Bai, the venerable figure who held the mantle of the village's senior elder, Rawal Nath peered deeply into the contours of her time-weathered face. A tapestry of expressive lines and deep-set shadows framed her countenance, her toothless smile accentuating the wisdom that seemed to emanate from her sunken cheeks.

As Gavri Bai began to speak, her words flowed forth with the compelling force of an unyielding river, her gestures embodying the enthusiasm of her narratives. Her storytelling was not just a recounting of events but a deep dive into the soul of the village and its inhabitants. She painted vivid, immersive tableaus, weaving a rich tapestry of age-old customs and legends that held Andrew and Candice in rapt attention.

"The enigmatic lore of the Banjara tribe," she proclaimed, her voice taking on an almost hypnotic quality, "runs as deep as the ancient roots of the trees. The spirits of our forebears linger among us, imparting profound truths to those willing to heed their whispers."

Beside her, Rawal Nath stood in respectful silence, enveloped by a profound sense of serenity, as the weight of centuries-old history and the ethereal presence of spirits infused the air around them.

As Gavri Bai turned to face him again, Rawal Nath could not wait any longer to ask his questions. They listened intently as the old woman shared her wisdom and reassurance, with Rawal Nath passionately translating for Andrew and Candice.

"The legend of Neelam Banjara has been passed down from generation to generation," Gavri Bai began. "I, too, have grown up singing songs about the forbidden love between Bhanwar and Neelam."

As she immersed herself further into the tale, Gavri Bai's expression shifted from wistful nostalgia to haunting distress. Her words carried a palpable weight as she vividly described the tragic events unfolding on that fateful day. Rawal Nath couldn't help but feel a shiver run down his spine as he translated the horror and profound sorrow in Gavri Bai's voice. The story held Andrew and Candice in rapt attention; their eyes widened, and their mouths slightly ajar, entirely captivated by the emotional intensity of Gavri Bai's narrative.

Chapter 13:

Buried Alive

"The soul can never be cut to pieces by any weapon, nor burned by fire, nor moistened by water, nor withered by the wind."

– Bhagwat Gita: Chapter Two, Verse 23

Chief Balchand's hand shook as he tightly clasped the worn hilt of his sword, feeling the cold, unyielding steel weighing on him like the burden of guilt and grief over his son Bhanwar's untimely passing. His weathered, calloused fingers traced the intricate carvings on the blade, symbolising the honour and duty that had shaped his life. His eyes blazed with a mix of fury, sorrow, and disbelief as they locked onto the woman accountable for this tragic turn of events.

Neelam lay before Chief Balchand, her broken ankle leaving her incapacitated and unable to bear her weight. The chief was overwhelmed with emotions, ranging from concern for Neelam to a sense of urgency. The dim torchlight flickered off the ancient stone walls, casting eerie and elongated shadows across the chamber. The tension in the air was palpable, making it feel as if the atmosphere crackled with an electric charge. In a voice that boomed through the air like thunder, King Balchand commanded his men with authority and determination, his words echoing off the cavernous walls.

"Take this woman away from here. But do not end her life. Let her instead be interred in my dungeon, used to soothe my anguish whenever I set foot above her. Seal her in a small chamber and seal it off with bricks. Choke her of air so she may die a slow, agonising death. May her pain match my sorrow until her last breath leaves her."

The soldiers acted swiftly, seizing Neelam with a firm grip on her arms while her hair billowed in the wind. Despite the pain, she bravely endured, her injured foot struggling to support her weight. The chief's urgent order cut through the air, commanding Vanshikha, his wife, to return to the camp. Balchand felt a pang of distress as he witnessed his wife's anguish, but he stoically maintained his composure, refusing to show any hint of vulnerability.

Turning then to the lifeless body of his son Bhanwar, Balchand's voice cracked as he gave orders to two soldiers, "Gather a small group and bring my son's body to our palace. He shall receive a funeral worthy of a Prince and my son." And with that, King Balchand left the clearing as the soldiers began their preparations to transport Bhanwar's body back home.

Sensing an opportune moment, Neelam's father gestured to his warriors hiding in the dense foliage.

With arrows and swords they quickly took down Balchand's soldiers who had remained behind to guard the prince's body. The Banjara chief stepped into the clearing, gestured at four loyalists, and commanded in an agonising voice.

"Take the prince's corpse and hide it until I can secure my daughter's release. Trading his body for her life is the only means to get her back alive."

His voice faded away as he paused, gazing upon his missing digits. With trembling hands, he removed his turban and wrapped it around what remained of his three mutilated fingers. One of his men had delicately picked up the bony stubs from the ground and secured them in a cloth.

The Banjara men rushed forward to collect the prince's body before hastily disappearing into the nearby bushes.

Nagarmal, his weathered face grim and determined, quickly rallied his troops and began devising a plan of attack. However, their plans were interrupted by the piercing screams echoing from the nearby village. Without hesitation, Nagarmal and his men charged towards the source of the chaos.

As they approached the village square, thick plumes of smoke filled their nostrils, and the sounds of crackling flames filled their ears. The sight that greeted them was enough to make even the bravest warrior's heart skip a beat: Balchand's forces mercilessly burning down homes and buildings while demanding the return of the prince's corpse.

Anger boiled within Nagarmal. The Banjara chief wasted no time acting and sprinted toward the soldiers, with his loyal villagers close behind him, armed with various weapons and tools.

With a fierce roar, Nagarmal lunged at one of the soldiers and hoisted him off the ground in his uniform. "Where have they taken my daughter?" His voice shook with fury. The soldier could barely choke out a response through his fear. "They have taken her by carriage to King Balchand's palace."

Nagarmal's scowl deepened, but he loosened his grip just enough for the soldier to utter one final warning. "You are foolish to think that they will trade. My king would sooner see her dead than give her up in exchange for his son's body."

Nagarmal's piercing eyes narrowed as he slowly drove his foot against the soldier's chest, grinding him into the soft soil beneath their feet. He then turned to his maternal cousin, Kishan Parmar, a seasoned fighter and loyal servant of the clan.

"Kishan, gather your most skilled men and rescue my precious daughter. Bring her back to me, please," Nagarmal pleaded urgently.

Kishan nodded solemnly, his jaw set in determination. He quickly rounded up two of his most muscular men, mounting them on powerful horses, before setting off frenzied towards Balchand's palace.

As they neared the imposing estate, Kishan and his men saw dozens of heavily armed guards lining the walls. They knew they would have to proceed cautiously to succeed in their mission. Carefully dismounting from their steeds, they held vigil nearby while keeping a close eye on the palace.

Kishan observed King Balchand in a lively discussion with men toting around exotic, unfamiliar gear. His sharp gaze followed the leader as he marched determinedly to a hidden courtyard nook and vanished into an underground vault. While Kishan's thoughts whirled, he pondered their sparse choices. Indeed, there was a secret portal to be found, yet as moments tumbled away like sand in an hourglass, the question loomed—could they uncover it before time ran out?

As they moved through the darkness, their footsteps barely making a sound, Kishan, and his companions knew the stakes were high. Kishan's eyes scanned the area, searching for any sign of King Balchand's guards. He could still feel the weight of the threat to "bury her alive" hanging in the air. They were outnumbered, and the odds were stacked against them, but they couldn't afford to hesitate. Neelam's life depended on their swift and decisive actions.

Pooling their thoughts and channelling their anger, the trio carefully devised a plan. Each movement was deliberate, and every word was exchanged in hushed tones. After subduing a few enemy soldiers, they took on their identities, using deception to navigate through enemy territory and reach the dungeon where Neelam was held captive.

The dungeon greeted them with its cold, oppressive atmosphere. The only light came from the flickering torches, casting eerie shadows on the damp stone walls. In the distance, the haunting echoes of Neelam's cries cut through the silence, spurring them on despite the fear that gripped their hearts. They followed the anguished sounds, drawing closer to the sight of Neelam being restrained and tormented by the king's men. Seeing her in such distress ignited a fierce determination within Kishan and his companions.

As they stood in the dimly lit corridor, the urgency of their mission weighed heavily on their shoulders. Neelam's suffering fuelled an unwavering resolve to rescue her. The air around them crackled with fear and determination as they prepared to face the impending confrontation. Their eyes locked, silent communication passing between them as they readied themselves to confront the oppressors and secure Neelam's freedom, no matter the cost.

King Balchand stood before Neelam's limp form, a towering figure like a bloodthirsty dragon preparing to breathe fire.

His words were laced with malice as he barked orders at his soldiers. "Quicken your pace! I want her sealed in that wall, left to die a slow and agonising death."

With a robust and determined kick, his boot struck the pile of weathered bricks, sending them tumbling down the narrow passage.

The sound of crumbling stone echoed through the air, and a fine cloud of dust filled every crevice and corner.

Neelam stood defiantly before her captors, her once bright and flowing dress now reduced to tatters, her body trembling from the cold and fear as they forcefully dragged her towards an ominous alcove.

The iron shackles that bound her wrists seared into her skin, leaving angry red marks in their wake. She fought against them with all her might, her eyes blazing with unyielding determination to break free from their relentless grip. But the soldiers were blinded by their cruelty, mistaking her courageous resistance for mere fear or desperation.

Among them, a young man with messy hair spilling out from beneath his turban saw through the facade. His eyes held a glimmer of empathy and understanding, betraying a kindness and compassion that set him apart from his callous companions.

But any shred of empathy he may have felt was shattered when Neelam bared her teeth and snarled like a wild animal, hurling curses at them until her last breaths: "May you all suffer and rot before your natural deaths."

The soldier's eyes bulged in shock, his steps faltering as he turned away from the broken figure before him. Neelam's body convulsed with deep anguish and injustice, ragged sobs escaping from her lips and tearing through the deafening silence.

The soldiers shifted uncomfortably under her piercing gaze as they secured her with heavy chains. With cold determination, they began to pile brick upon brick, constructing a barrier around her like a fortress. As the wall gradually reached up to her knees, Neelam's screams echoed through the air with a fiery rage.

"May you and your descendants be cursed for all eternity! Your name will forever be synonymous with cruelty and malice, spoken with venomous disgust by all who hear it. You may take my life, but know that the memory of your heinous deeds will live on through the ages!"

Neelam's voice reverberated with raw, unbridled emotion, dripping with venom and seething hatred that seemed to radiate a searing heat. Even the most stoic soldiers quivered in fear, their faces twisted into masks of fury as they confronted her. Balchand's putrid saliva dripped down her bloodied cheek as he spat at her, every movement of his contorted body betraying his intense rage.

Against the unforgiving stone walls of her prison, Neelam unleashed a scream of such ferocity that it felt as though the very foundations of the building trembled. The soldiers, driven by the sheer terror of her unyielding power, hastily erected a barrier to separate themselves from the raging woman. One brick after another was stacked, creating a wall that effectively sealed Neelam within her living tomb. Still, even behind the barrier, her piercing screams persisted, haunting reminders of her indomitable spirit and unwavering defiance against oppression.

Neelam's piercing screams reverberated through the dank stone walls of her prison cell. Though her body was trapped behind bricks and mortar, her indomitable voice could not be contained. The soldiers, panicked by her raw power, scrambled to finish the makeshift wall, their fear urging them to work faster.

They stacked the heavy bricks individually, shutting out the light until only a thin sliver remained. Neelam's fiery eyes blazed through the narrow opening, striking fear into the soldiers' hearts. She unleashed another bone-chilling scream, and the men stumbled back, bricks tumbling from their trembling hands.

The scene was tense as the commanding officer barked orders, desperate to stifle Neelam's unwavering voice. With shaky hands, the soldiers swiftly cemented the final bricks in place, engulfing Neelam in an ominous silence within the confines of the dungeon. The soldiers stood motionless, straining to catch any hint of a sound emanating from Neelam's tomb. For a moment, it appeared that her spirit had been crushed.

Subsequently, a profound and measured chant began to permeate the gaps within the brickwork. Neelam's sonorous tones vibrated with steadfast force and resolve. The troops were enveloped by a wave of unease as her bold tune rose, unaffected by barriers of masonry and metal. Her indomitable spirit persisted, transcending the physical barriers intended to contain her.

The three Banjara men, their faces obscured and filled with fear, exchanged desperate glances as they stood before the imposing dungeon entrance. With a subtle gesture, Kishan directed them to silently retreat up the dim, moisture-laden passage into a small alcove. Faced with an agonising choice, Kishan felt the weight of responsibility to keep his men safe. But leaving Neelam behind weighed heavily on his heart, knowing that she would be left to confront almost certain death alone. As they departed, he silently prayed to the powers to grant her enough air in the confined space to endure until he could rally reinforcements and set her free.

Neelam's high-pitched wailing suddenly ceased, leaving an unsettling void amid the chaos. The abrupt transition to eerie silence sent shivers down the spines of Balchand's soldiers as if the very air had been sucked out of their lungs. One of the soldiers, hesitant yet compelled, cautiously approached the final layer of bricks and dared to peek through the slim gap. What met his gaze was a haunting sight - Neelam's lifeless form, suspended in a macabre stillness, her head hung low and eyes closed. A wave of conflicting emotions engulfed him as he struggled to muster the courage to confirm what he already knew. With a heavy heart, he called out to his comrades, his voice laden with a mix of relief and despair, "She is gone... she has departed this world."

Trembling hands reached out to place the last bricks in their rightful place, sealing Neelam inside forever.

Balchand's blood boiled with anger and frustration as he pounded on the wall in anger at Neelam's passing. He had wanted her to be bricked up alive in this crypt and then die from a lack of oxygen – a slow, agonising death. Even though Neelam had suffered immensely, Balchand's cruelty was not satisfied.

Meanwhile, Kishan could not bear to watch anymore and turned away, slowly retreating towards the dungeon entrance. His two companions followed, their faces sombre.

Once they stepped outside the magnificent palace, Kishan's pained expression betrayed his guilt and remorse. "How will I ever face our chief and deliver the devastating news of Neelam's demise?" he exclaimed, his voice quivering with emotion. He shook his head in disbelief. "We cannot stand idle. We must hasten back to our village and muster a formidable force to reclaim what remains of Neelam." Without a moment's delay, they swiftly mounted their sturdy horses and embarked on their solemn journey towards the Banjara village, their hearts burdened with an unyielding mix of sorrow and resolve.

When they returned to the village, Nagarmal looked at them and intuitively knew something was wrong. He collapsed onto the ground, sobbing uncontrollably. Through his tears, he pleaded with

Kishan, "Where is my daughter's body? I must cremate her to release her soul."

Kishan fought back his tears as he explained that Neelam had been buried in an alcove within a dungeon of Balchand's palace, and all they could do was wait and see what would happen next.

Beneath the shadow of furrowed brows, Nagarmal nestled his deep sorrow, submerged in his ocean of desolation without uttering a word. Observing this, Kishan signalled the others to give him room for mourning, an expanse where his tears could cascade freely and his anguish reign in solemn solitude.

In his isolation, Nagarmal's figure was etched against the stillness, his palm pressed to his heart as if to quell the unrelenting sting of deep-rooted grief. Inwardly, he gazed upon Neelam's visage, his daughter, whose lustre brought unabashed pride and joy into his life – his cherished jewel. The vicious hands of destiny that wrenched her away so ruthlessly laid a sorrowful weight upon his spirit. Visions of her trapped in a dank and dreadful cell played across his mind, coupled with the terror she must have endured. The love that pulsed from a father's essence now battled with a tide of inconsolable sorrow.

Recollections of Prince Bhanwar, whose life had tragically become intertwined with Neelam's, stirred a hidden curse within Nagarmal's soul. Despite his lingering suspicions, the harsh reality they faced surpassed his worst fears. The lovers' wedding haunted him, fuelling his animosity towards the ruler, King Balchand. With each breath, he heard whispers of curses and felt a genuine desire for revenge against the oppressive monarch consuming his mind.

Nagarmal's knees gave way as he pleaded for divine grace for his beloved's peaceful passage into the afterlife. Regret ate away at him, his heart yearning for one last glimpse of her face, one final embrace, and a chance to express his boundless love. Yet, he found himself trapped by the unforgiving grip of memory, engulfed in sorrow, while an unyielding thirst for vengeance against the mighty Bhati overlord, Nagarmal, raged within him.

Chapter 14:

The Secret in the Dungeon

"If you prick us, do we not bleed? If you tickle us, do we not laugh? If you poison us, do we not die? And if you wrong us, shall we not revenge?"

– The Merchant of Venice, Act 3, Scene 1
by William Shakespeare

Every person in the room listened intently as the ancient woman relayed her story. Candice couldhardly contain her shock and grief.

"Andrew," she said, her voice trembling with emotion, "they entombed her alive! They bricked her inside so that she would starve or suffocate to death. That is inhuman."

Candice slowly turned to face Commissioner Prabhat, her eyes filled with determination. "So where exactly is this Palace of the Bhatis located, and how do we reach it?" she inquired, her voice betraying a hint of impatience.

Commissioner Prabhat furrowed his brow momentarily before asking the elderly woman, Gavri Bai, for directions. She smiled softly and pointed towards the distant horizon. "It lies on the banks of

Soor Sagar Lake," she replied, her words carrying a sense of reverence for the place.

Commissioner Prabhat relayed the information to his brother Pranay, who informed them that the palace was just two kilometres away. He also warned them to exercise caution, as the Bhati family had long since abandoned the palace due to sickness and misfortune. Parts of the building were now in ruins or had been reconstructed, making it difficult to predict what they might find upon arrival.

Commissioner Prabhat's eyes narrowed as he pulled Candice and Andrew aside, his voice urgent and serene. "We must speak to Vaibhav Bhati at once," he whispered, "we need his permission to enter the old palace."

Candice nodded, her mind already racing through all the scenarios. Acting quickly, she dialled Vaibhav's number and updated him on their situation. She could feel the intensity of his excitement through the phone line as she spoke.

Commissioner Prabhat's eyes narrowed as he pulled Candice and Andrew aside, his voice urgent and serene. "We must speak to Vaibhav Bhati at once," he whispered, "we need his permission and support to enter the old palace."

Candice nodded, her mind already racing through all the scenarios. She took out her phone and dialled Vaibhav's number, hoping he would answer. After a few rings, she heard his voice on the other end. "Hello, Candice. What's the latest?" he asked eagerly.

"Candice spoke with her voice steady and business-like, but inside, she was a storm of nerves and buzzing energy. "Vaibhav, we're on to something big. We suspect that Neelam and Prince Bhanwar's remains may be concealed within the dark catacombs or hidden alcoves of your family's historic abode in Soor Sagar – the ancient stronghold of the Bhatis. We can hasten to your estate anytime now, yet we require your authorisation to enter and someone from inside to guide our steps at the entrance. Can we count on you for this?"

Vaibhav absorbed every word intensely, sensing the electric charge behind her measured words. He offered, "You forge ahead to the main threshold of the estate, and I will ensure everything is in place for your arrival," his voice thoughtful as he spurred them into action.

The group's anticipation was palpable as they piled into their minibus. Candice could not shake off a sudden unease as they drove towards their destination. How had she suddenly become so invested in this investigation? Pushing aside her doubts, she focused on the task at hand.

The trip was short and without incident, leading them directly to the regal doors of the palace. They were greeted by a compact man named Yusuf, who offered his introduction at the entrance. However, the air around her ensnared Candice's senses as she alighted from their carriage. It hung heavy with the echoes of tales untold, beckoning her to explore its hidden depths.

As Yusuf's hand wrought the ancient padlock on the massive iron gate open with an old, tarnished key, a shiver of uncertainty echoed through Candice like a cold whisper. Yet, there was no retreating; they were bound by their decision, past the point of no return.

Their advance towards the ominous edifice felt like wading through shadows, each step laden with a growing sense of foreboding. The crunch of dried foliage and dust underfoot accompanied their procession up the winding drive, flanked on one side by cobblestones peeking through sporadic clumps of ashen grass.

Upon reaching the mansion's imposing threshold, Candice caught her breath in an audible intake, awe mingling with apprehension in her exclamation. "How majestic," she exhaled in wonder.

Her companions offered mute concurrence, heads bobbing wordlessly as Yusuf swung the door open with a gesture that seemed to beckon the past back into the light. Inside lay a dishevelled tableau: furniture tossed asunder, shrouded in once-white cloths now baptised in the grime of ages. The dusty footprints that crisscrossed the hall gave the unsettling impression of presence where there should be none.

Andrew cleared his throat and tapped Yusuf on the shoulder, addressing him urgently. "Yusuf, we need to find the dungeons below this palace. Can you lead us there?"

Yusuf's frown deepened as he replied defensively, "Dungeon? I've worked here for thirty years, and there has never been a dungeon here." His stance was firm and resolute, and he was unsure whether to show them around or ask them to leave altogether.

Andrew's face grew more perplexed as he scanned the chaotic scene. "Well then," he said slowly, "perhaps there is some secret chamber hidden within these walls?"

Yusuf's eyes lit up with sudden realisation. "Ah, you must mean the old underground tank built here in the 1970s!" he exclaimed.

Uncertainty clawed at Andrew's mind as he followed Yusuf through the poorly illuminated courtyard, his heart pounding with anticipation and unease. His insatiable curiosity propelled him onward, though lingering doubts weighed heavily on his thoughts. They arrived at a secluded courtyard corner where a worn, metal hatch lay in the ground. Andrew swung open the hatch with a decisive tug, exposing an eerie dark tank filled with motionless, deep water. A tiny lizard scuttled along the tank's wall before vanishing into the murky depths below. It struggled fruitlessly to regain its foothold on the damp walls, setting the once-calm surface into undulating waves. Startled, Candice recoiled, but Andrew couldn't resist the urge to peer closer, squinting to discern concealed mysteries within the turbid waters.

As Andrew brushed off his hands and feet, he noticed Candice scowling at her phone. Her frustration was palpable in her fervent discussion with Vaibhav regarding their lack of headway in discovering hidden dungeons or secret chambers within the palace. Just as she pocketed her phone, she seized Andrew's arm urgently and leaned in closely to whisper firmly and urgently in his ear.

"Do you remember that mysterious man we saw at Baba Kanmal's? The one who warned us to stay away while waving a dagger in our faces?"

Confusion etched into Andrew's expression as he nodded slowly. "Why are you bringing him up now?"

Candice's gaze shifted towards the entrance gate. "I swear I just saw him lurking behind the bars of the front gate, looking in on us!"

A shiver ran down Andrew's spine as he, too, caught a glimpse of a figure clad in all black before it disappeared again. The hairs on his neck stood on end as he realised they were not alone in their search for answers.

A nervous sound of reassurance escaped Andrew's lips, but it was quickly stifled by a thick plume of smoke rising outside the gate and expanding, darkening the sky. Candice's eyes widened in questioning fear as they rushed to join Commissioner Prabhat and Pranay at the scene. The minibus was ablaze, with flames dancing wildly through the open windows. Yusuf and the security guard shouted for help, but their efforts were in vain as the fire relentlessly consumed the vehicle.

The roar of the flames hummed in the air as the minibus became enveloped in a ferocious inferno. The fire surged upwards, casting a menacing glow against the darkening sky and sending sparks and billows of thick black smoke spiralling into the air. A searing heat washed over Candice, Andrew, Prabhat, and Pranay, scorching their skin and searing their lungs as they stood transfixed, their eyes locked on the voracious fire as it consumed everything in its path. The crackling and hissing of the flames seemed to echo with an insatiable hunger, showing no mercy as it relentlessly devoured all in its wake.

Shattered glass became lethal projectiles, propelled by the violent force of the fire. The rubber tyres melted into pools of sticky tar, and the once sturdy metal frame twisted and contorted under the relentless assault of scorching heat. At that moment, hope seemed to evaporate as Candice and her companions stood in helpless dismay, their hearts heavy with dread, as they realised their sole means of escape had been reduced to charred remnants.

Was this a natural disaster or an act of intentional arson? They were facing a cruel fate at the hands of a ruthless enemy – fire and possibly another enemy, the arsonist.

Candice trembled in fear, her eyes fixed on the inferno raging before her. Andrew's face contorted with fury, his body trembling with a fierce determination. He let out a guttural cry like a bull ready to charge. His gaze hardened when he caught sight of human figures lurking in the bushes across the street. They wore masks and turbans, but it was clear that they had a hand in the torching of the minibus.

Something inside Andrew snapped; he grabbed fistfuls of large rocks from the ground and launched them at the fleeing figures, spewing obscenities with each throw. One stone struck a burly man square in the back, causing him to stumble and fall face-first into a deep ditch.

A sharp cry of pain echoed through the air, sending shivers down Candice's spine. Blood gushed from a deep wound on his thigh, where a thick iron rod had pierced through his flesh and bone. The rod was one of many that protruded from the ground, ready to reinforce the concrete foundations of a new building. The man had landed on a pile of bricks, rubble, and metal scraps, which added to his injuries and agony.

Commissioner Prabhat and Pranay arrived at the scene together; their faces paled with shock as they took in the gruesome sight.

They slowly descended into the pit. As they reached the injured man, their eyes were drawn to the large iron rod that had impaled his thigh and the pool of blood dripping down the iron rod to an ever-growing crimson streak in the dust.

Andrew stood motionless at the edge of the pit, his chest heaving as he stared down at the man he had struck. The initial surge of rage that had compelled him slowly subsided, leaving him shaken. "What have I done?" The thought rang in his head.

Candice watched from above with fear and concern as Andrew scrambled down. With great care, they manoeuvred the injured man off the iron rod. Using a makeshift tourniquet, Andrew ripped off the man's turban to staunch blood flow. The fabric quickly became soaked with blood.

Candice stood paralysed, unable to tear her eyes away from the dark puddle of blood that had seeped into the dry earth at the foot of the iron rod. She had never seen such anguish, such pain. Bile rose in her throat. They started moving him from the pit's bottom to the top.

Candice watched in horror as Commissioner Prabhat, Pranay, and Andrew struggled to lift the wailing man from the pit. His agonised screams pierced the arid air as they carefully manoeuvred his limp body over the pit's edge. Fresh blood poured from his mangled thigh, soaking through the hastily tied tourniquet.

Without warning, three figures emerged from the shadows, their hands held up in a sign of submission. They cautiously approached their wounded comrade with fear etched on their faces. As they helped move him to the side of the lonely road, a rickety bus careened into view, its engine sputtering and gasping for life.

With panicked passengers leaping to their feet and shouting in terror, the group struggled to board the decrepit vehicle. Andrew's once-white shirt now hung heavily with deep crimson stains, contrasting sharply against the bleak surroundings. The driver, his face twisted with suspicion, blocked their path and refused to aid them, insisting they call the authorities instead. His eyes darted between the injured man and the surrounding group as he demanded answers.

Andrew pleaded with the driver, "Please, we need your help. This man is gravely hurt. Can you take us to the nearest hospital?" gesturing towards the bleeding figure on the roadside. But the driver shook his head vehemently. "No, no, I can't do that. You should call the police. This looks like a crime scene. Who are you people, and what are you doing here?" His voice grew more agitated with each question.

Frustration surged through Andrew as he tried to reason with the driver. "We are not criminals. We are on an investigation," he explained while pointing to Commissioner Prabhat beside him, a badge glinting in the dim light. "He can vouch for us later. Right now, this man's life is at stake, and we need to get him medical attention immediately." He motioned for their group to enter the bus and continue stemming the flow of blood from their companion's wounds.

The driver hesitated, fear warring with curiosity in his wary gaze. "I don't know...this seems too risky," he muttered nervously. "What if you're lying? What if you're involved in something illegal? What if the real police catch me, and I lose my job, my freedom, everything?" His voice trembled as he considered the consequences.

It was only when Commissioner Prabhat revealed his identity as a high-ranking police officer that the driver finally relented and agreed to take them. With a quick motion of his weapon, the Commissioner ordered the three men who had emerged from hiding to share what they knew. The group stared fearfully at the gun pointed their way but complied with shaking hands. Once he had gathered all the necessary information, Commissioner Prabhat holstered his weapon and turned towards Andrew and Candice with grim determination in his eyes.

"These three were part of a mission to stop us from finding the bodies of the two lovers," he explained gravely. "Their original plan was to scare us, but now Badri's, the injured man, injury has turned things around. We must hurry and get Badri to a hospital. He is likely to die from loss of blood if not treated in time. Oh, and Badri is Brother Rajesh's son and the same person who threatened us with a knife as we were leaving the Banjara temple yesterday."

Abruptly, one of the Banjara men in black clothing handed Commissioner Prabhat a mobile phone. After speaking in rapid, short sentences, he revealed that he had just spoken to Brother Rajesh, the elder from the Banjara temple. It was confirmed that the wounded man was indeed Brother Rajesh's son, Badri.

Minutes later, they were in the Mahatma Gandhi Hospital emergency ward in Jodhpur. The arrival hall was hot and oppressive, full of people pacing and murmuring. Some were crying, some were shouting, some were praying. The air conditioning was not working, and the fans only circulated the stale and suffocating air. Candice felt sweat trickling down her back as she pushed through the crowd. She hoped they would find a doctor soon for Badri, who was losing consciousness. Candice's phone startled her with its insistent metallic chime. It was Vaibhav calling. She passed the phone to Andrew, praying he could solve their dilemma as he had an animated discussion with Vaibhav. Andrew grabbed a pen and paper from the nurse sitting at the reception, who looked harried and overwhelmed by the influx of patients. He returned shortly afterwards with news that gave them a glimmer of hope.

"I have information. The dungeon was closed off a hundred years ago. It's unclear why this was done, but someone wanted to seal it off permanently. The entrance is from the left of the main gate, but they put cobblestones over it. We must look for a circle of black stone. Dig under these stones, and we will find the old entrance to the dungeon."

Commissioner Prabhat, Pranay, and Andrew discussed this development, but Candice refused to go immediately, citing exhaustion. They returned to the Gladwell residence for sustenance before heading out again with Sandhya. Her fractured arm was a constant reminder of the danger ahead.

Yusuf's furrowed brow and tense demeanour met the group as they neared the regal structure.

A scorched minibus hauntingly marred the palace entryway, stark against the ornate construction. Yet, Pranay remained unshaken, steeling himself for the impending challenge. Four burly workers gleamed with sweat in the sun's glare, toiling industriously with their shining implements, handpicked by Commissioner Prabhat to unearth the mysteries beneath the ground.

Barking orders, Yusuf prompted a worker to fetch brooms briskly. However, the rising dust swirled so thickly that it choked their breaths. Two of the crew masked their faces with cloths, returning to their sweep with the rigour of possessed men. After long minutes of rigorous excavation, Pranay's voice erupted in victory, beckoning his allies to observe. Engraved brown tiles lay ensconced in filth, woven into elaborate designs. He signalled carefully to the workers, who sprang into action with precision, levering up the heavy stones to the rhythm of descending into the earth. Then, a strident 'clang!' reverberated as a pickaxe revealed a covert passageway furnished with an archaic ringed handle.

The quartet of workers heaved in harmony, wrenching the door, which released a groaning protest and gave rise to billowing dust plumes. An ominous void now unveiled itself, enticing and unsettling. Commissioner Prabhat equipped Andrew with a torch, igniting another for himself, encouraging them to pierce the spectral depths below. As they forged onward, the stink of decay and an oppressive air of trepidation filled their senses. Nonetheless, they advanced into the enveloping shadow, bracing themselves for the secrets shrouded in the murk.

As Andrew descended, a swell of warmth enveloped him, carrying the mingling scents of coal and dust. Around him, large kitchen implements were scattered in disarray, looming next to mountains of sooty coal. The room below opened dramatically; its walls pocketed with niches that cradled countless trinkets and curious items.

Andrew absorbed the scene, unfurling in the soft glow of scant light. The space was lined with shelving, each heaving under the weight of peculiar keepsakes: boxes etched with elaborate patterns, swords with a sinister sheen, and shields with arcane symbols. He meandered along the central pathway, eyes flitting from one shadowed recess to another, spying the layers of time displayed as dust and spiderwebs over forgotten relics.

His gaze was inexorably drawn to a sealed niche at the room's furthest reach. An unsettling sensation washed over him, a suspicion that Neelam rested within that bricked enclosure. His gut twisted with apprehension. Mere steps behind, Candice and the Charan brothers also tentatively descended into the depths.

Candice's voice cut through the silence just as his mind wandered. "Wait! Look behind us; there is another bricked-up alcove. Could there be two bodies here? Could it be both Bhanwar and Neelam?"

Her words sent shivers down the spines of the four labourers who had accompanied them. They were alarmed at the notion of dead bodies being present in the dark dungeon. Commissioner Prabhat quickly stepped in to calm them down and ordered them to start chipping away at the bricks of the first alcove.

The group stood rooted in horror, their eyes wide with shock as they surveyed the scene before them. The once sturdy walls were now reduced to rubble, bricks scattered haphazardly on the ground. Yusuf's hand trembled uncontrollably around his umbrella, his voice shaking with disbelief and anger as he demanded to know who could have caused such destruction.

Commissioner Prabhat shot back at him sternly, warning him to stay back and let the police handle the situation. But Yusuf was too consumed by his emotions, barking orders at the terrified labourers to carefully remove the debris and uncover the source of the pungent smell that grew more powerful by the second.

As each brick was removed, Andrew's flashlight revealed a dark and damp passageway beyond. The tension in the air thickened, almost suffocating, as one of the labourers forcefully dug a pickaxe into the wall, resulting in a loud crack that sent shivers down everyone's spine.

Panic gripped all four men as they scattered in different directions, startled by the clanking of chains and the sudden appearance of a skeleton tumbling forward before coming to rest on the ground. Its skull rolled across the floor with an eerie creak, adding to the chaos and terror that filled the room.

The labourers did not pause even to scream, and with imaginary apparitions in their minds, they ran wildly back out the passage. Watching this, Pranay darted after the fleeing workers as well, while Yusuf remained frozen in shock, unable to move from his spot. Andrew stumbled forward, his hands trembling, as he reached out to examine the bones sprawled out before him. Sandhya hesitantly approached her father's side, mesmerised and petrified by this unexpected discovery.

Andrew's voice cracked with exhilaration and disbelief as he spoke, his tone revealing the profound astonishment brought on by the extraordinary sight before them. The dungeon was cloaked in an oppressive aura of dread, keeping everyone in unease as they endeavoured to make sense of the grim enigma before them. Amidst this atmosphere, the question persisted: Could this ancient skeleton hold the answers to unlocking the long-concealed secrets of this ominous place? Could this be Neelam?

He turned excitedly to the others and exclaimed, "Prabhat, Candice, I think we have found her! Good God!"

Candice and Commissioner Prabhat were flooded with relief at this revelation. But suddenly, Commissioner

Prabhat noticed something that caused him to cry a little. "Wait, this can't be her! Look at this - it is a skeleton wearing male battle armour. It has two feet, but Neelam severely damaged one foot, right? What is going on here?"

Their balloon of optimism stood deflated.

Suddenly, Candice, moving her light around the chamber, saw a glint that caught her eye. She walked over to what seemed to be an alcove bricked up with different-coloured mortar and misshaped bricks.

The two men were still rattled by the disappointment of finding a skeleton that was not Sandhya's. They whirled around to confront the bricked-up alcove looming behind them. Their hearts pounded furiously in their chests, a tumultuous mixture of fear and adrenaline coursing through their veins. With eyes wide and breaths held, they witnessed Candice frantically pushing aside loose bricks, her determination evident in her sweat-drenched hair and panicked expression. Andrew's gaze flitted around, desperately searching for Pranay and the four missing labourers who had been with them just moments ago but were now nowhere to be found. Without a second thought, he seized two heavy pickaxes and began relentlessly attacking the wall with all his strength. Commissioner Prabhat joined in, their combined efforts chiselling away at the solid brick-like two resolute ants confronting an imposing obstacle. Suddenly, a faint glimmer amidst the flying chunks of brick caught their attention - an array of chains, yet nobody connected to them. Disappointed but fuelled by an even stronger determination, they pressed on with their frantic search until Candice's voice cut through the chaos. Her revelation of a small hole near chest level rekindled their hope again. Shattering bricks reverberated through the air as they enlarged the gap, poised to uncover long-concealed secrets.

"There's another skeleton here," she exclaimed.

Andrew and the Commissioner quickly joined her in clearing away more bricks until they exposed the bones of a corpse pressed into the dirt. As Andrew shone his light on the remains, it was clear that whoever this person was had been laid down with care and dignity. He noticed a glimmer of gold from a dagger and a small open wooden box lying on the musty floor next to the skeleton. But as he looked closer, he realised that both feet were still intact - this was not the missing Banjara girl.

Andrew handed the flashlight to Candice as he examined the box further. What he saw inside frightened even him—there were coins and trinkets, but three pieces of ivory were lying in the box. Closer inspection led Andrew to whisper that these were human fingers sliced off by a sharp object. Andrew was appalled at the sight. Charan moved closer, equally taken aback but trying to understand what might have happened. Just then, Pranay and the four labourers returned. Andrew held up the three finger-like pieces for all to see and asked.

"What do you think this is? Looks like human fingers to me."

The group gasped in unison at what they saw and looked at each other in subdued confirmation of Andrew's assertion. Candice stepped back, her face pale with fear, as Andrew reached for a ring in the box. It was a gold ring with a roaring lion carved into it.

"Wait! I have seen this before," Yusuf said, sidling up to Andrew. "This belongs to the royal family. Give it to me so I can return it to its rightful owners."

Andrew yelled at Yusuf at the mere suggestion, "If this is a royal family ring, could it be that we just found it in the burial chamber of one of their ancestors?"

Yusuf snorted indignantly and replied, "This is a good Hindu family. They would never bury their own. They burn their dead according to Hindu funeral rites."

Commissioner Prabhat had been silent during all of this, squatting down as he held his torch and thought about the implications of this discovery. Suddenly, he spoke up, an idea coming to him in a wild moment of insight.

"We know that the Prince killed himself with a dagger, and King Balchand cut off three fingers from the Banjara chief."

Andrew reflected on this. "So, someone thought it was appropriate to bring these two items into the afterlife?" he questioned as they started to move away.

When they rose to the surface, the four labourers were seen talking to each other in the distance while washing their hands and feet with a tap.

Suddenly, Candice froze. She clutched at Andrew and blurted out, "I would wager a fortune that we just found Prince Bhanwar's corpse! Something is amiss here, or somebody reorganised history to confuse us and other explorers."

Everyone stared at each other, bewildered by what they had unearthed. What had they come across? Candice continued, "The other body is that of a soldier. I'm not sure that is connected to Neelam. It may be just another incident of barbery on Balchand's part, a red herring that confuses us. Focus on the skeleton with the dagger; that is the real deal!"

The group listened carefully. No one offered an alternate opinion.

Chapter 15:

The Cruel Swap

"The soul is never born nor dies at any time. The soul has not come into being, does not come into being, and will not. The soul is unborn, eternal, ever-existing, and primaeval. The soul is not slain when the body is slain."

– Bhagwat Gita, Chapter Two, Verse 20

Commissioner Prabhat took great care to ensure the security of the palace. He even made plans to retrieve the skeletons. After their journey, Candice suggested taking a break to rest, considering how tired the group was. On the other hand, Andrew felt restless and couldn't stop thinking about the mystery of their attacker and recent events. Full of curiosity, Charan was ready to question the injured assailant to unravel the story behind the mysterious events.

Dawn's light brought news from Commissioner Prabhat to Andrew; informants at the hospital stood ready to unveil their roles during the fray. With Candice, Andrew consented to wend their way to the institution. An air of tension hung like mist as they threaded through Jodhpur's vibrant maze.

Reaching the medical sanctuary, Charan and his entourage convened discreetly in an alcove, joined by a select coterie. Amongst them were two figures allied with the Banjara temple – the sage Baba Kanmal and Brother Rajesh, father to their attacker, who was also the lead instigator for setting the minibus on fire.

Baba Kanmal's discomfort was evident; he floundered with his wording, his eyes flickering in search of compassion from Candice's piercing scrutiny. She presented a visage of unwavering determination, internally grappling with the revelation of Baba Kanmal's unanticipated duplicity. Wrath simmered within her – how could a confidante weave such deceit? "Clarify yourself! What of Sandhya's injuries, the slain cat, the scorched conveyance of Pranay?" she interjected vehemently.

The contrite sage implored with joined hands, seeking absolution. "Brother Rajesh's actions harbour explanations. The girl's injury was unintended. Our warning meant to disrupt your dalliance with awakening those who slumber in eternity," he confessed.

Andrew stepped forward with a stern expression. "So, you orchestrated all these events? Tell me why you are here!" he demanded.

With a subtle gesture, Baba Kanmal acknowledged the situation and shifted his attention to Brother Rajesh, who was perched nearby and quivering with palpable distress. As tears carved silent trails down his cheeks, he offered a remorseful narrative of past deeds, revealing a saga riddled with deception that upended the Gladwell team's pursuit of truth.

"The solemn vow made before King Nagarmal by my forebears was one of vengeance for our Banjara kinswoman Neelam, slain by the merciless Chief Balchand. They concealed Prince Balchand's remains in rebellion, bargaining chips for Neelam's life. Alas, my ancestor Kishan bore witness to Neelam's grim fate as she was entombed alive within a clandestine, underground chamber."

Interrupting with impatience, Andrew sought clarity. "But what events brought the Prince's body to rest in the crypt, and who ferried Neelam's earthly remains away?"

Then, Candice articulated her disbelief amidst the unfolding theatre—a reverberating echo of astonishment over the orchestrated hindrances. "The lengths you, Brother Rajesh, sided by your son, took to swerve us from this path are astounding. Do you never mind engaging us in open dialogue and sharing your reasoning?" She punctuated her sentiment with a vigorous shake of her head, exacerbating the gravity of her dismay. Her critique poured forth, "The incident that befell Sandhya is indefensible, and yet you persisted in obstinance even after its consequence—and only when harm visited Badri, leaving him hospitalised, did the winds change course."

Like a statue, Andrew absorbed Candice's narrative. Beside him, Rajesh gathered a solemn nod, a canvas of remorse across his features.

"Our aim was never to cause harm; the intent was merely to rattle you," he admitted with a heavy heart. "Learning of your journey towards the palace sent us into a tailspin—you were on the verge of unearthing the Prince's hidden remains." His words dwindled into a whisper of sorrow. "Your bravery and swift action saved my child. For this reason, I've laid bare the truth before you."

At that moment, a physician emerged at the entryway, beckoning Commissioner Prabhat aside for a brief exchange. He rejoined with news in tow. "Badri has transcended peril," he relayed. "He welcomes visitors in his sanctuary of recovery, though briefly, for his strength is yet returning."

Treading in the wake of Commissioner Prabhat and their guide, Candice and Andrew traversed the corridor, each footfall echoing with the sad weight of a looming confrontation. They paused before a door marked "Private Ward," the air thick with anticipation as they prepared to face the unknown.

As the group entered, Badri's face was etched with astonishment. The formidable ghost from his nightmares was now flesh and blood before him, flanked by those he once hunted. Remorse washed over him as he clasped his hands together, seeking silent forgiveness from these accidental adversaries.

The venerable Rajesh mirrored this silent appeal, coaxing empathy from the gathering to absolve past grievances. But Commissioner Prabhat cut through the moment with pragmatism, inquiring about

Badri's return to full strength. And then, Rajesh cast out a tantalising enigma to Andrew and Candice—could they postpone, for another week, the pursuit of Neelam, the Banjara maiden dormant for three centuries? They could then have Badri join them in retrieving Neelam's remains. The revelation rippled through the room, leaving behind a resonant shock.

Hope filled Candice's gaze, pivoting towards Andrew, whose translation came like a beacon: "He claims he knows final Neelam's resting place!" Expectations hung in the air as everyone leaned forward, thirsting for more.

Commissioner Prabhat, slicing through the suspense, demanded, "Disclose the location, and we shall embark on the retrieval. Is she concealed or interred?" The elder's head bobbed earnestly. With a gulp, he embarked on the haunting odyssey of Neelam, injecting life into a saga older than ages, backtracking to the moment Nagarmal learned of his child's fate in the shadows of a dungeon.

The gentle rotation of an old ceiling fan broke the stillness in the room, its blades creating a soothing hum. Candice and Andrew stood facing each other, their faces mirroring the uncertainty they felt inside as they listened raptly.

Chapter 16:

Protected in Death

The only reason why people have such death fears is that they know nothing beyond the body.

– Sadhguru

The sorrowful howl that Nagarmal erupted when he learned of Neelam's untimely passing pierced the very essence of his devoted warriors and the townsfolk. His words fractured with emotion as he faced Kishan, his trusted confidant and counsellor.

"Kishan," he prayed, "it is imperative that we recover Neelam's departed form to honour her memory with dignity. Her spirit yearns for tranquillity and a fitting farewell. Could we not petition King Balchand for an exchange and close this mournful tale?"

Affixed in silent reverence, Kishan was engulfed by profound loss and seething rage for what had become of Neelam. Since her days of youth, he had watched over her, witnessing her transformation into a benevolent soul whose mere presence was a beacon of happiness in their hamlet. But fate had cruelly claimed her, robbed of her years by a vile tyrant's hands. As Neelam's once vibrant grin and mirthful chuckles haunted his thoughts, they tore at his heartstrings even more fiercely. Yet, Kishan knew he must rise above the tides of grief - there remained a cause of justice to uphold in Neelam's name.

Suddenly, the sound of Nagarmal's words cut through the fog of Kishan's reverie, anchoring him back into the stark reality before him. At that moment, he recognised how deeply he had been submerged in his sorrow. With renewed resolve lighting his gaze, Kishan locked eyes with Nagarmal, a silent vow igniting within him. His anguish transformed into resolve. Kishan was now driven by a singular quest – to right the wrongs done to Neelam and to honour her memory by ensuring retribution.

With a swift brush of his hand, Kishan banished the trails of tears from his cheeks. His face set into a mould of resolute granite. The thought of rest was banished until justice could cradle Neelam's memory. Though her absence formed a chasm of pain that threatened to consume him, Kishan fortified his spirit with courage. Moving forward, he stepped into solidarity with Nagarmal and their fellow villagers huddled at the fringe of the woods. Their faces were maps of shared torment and fury; Neelam's gentle essence had touched each life profoundly. Her laughter, which once danced like a vivid melody through their homes, her silhouette a fleeting shadow of innocence, was cruelly plucked from this world too soon by the hands of malice.

As Kishan's mind wandered back, he could vividly recall when he had shared Neelam's first taste of a jalebi with her. The sugary spirals of the treat were still warm from the vendor's cart, and the look of joy on Neelam's face was as radiant as the star-studded sky above them. She savoured the syrupy coils, leaving a glistening circle upon her smiling lips. Kishan yearned for just one more fleeting glimpse of that pure happiness. But those cherished days had now faded into mere shadows, leaving only the challenging path ahead.

With unwavering determination, Kishan steeled himself, suppressing the looming wave of grief. The memory of Neelam's infectious laughter would now be his guiding light as he and his kin delved into the forest's embrace, bound together in their quest for retribution. Their mission was fuelled by love for the beloved girl, whose bright grin was permanently etched in Kishan's heart.

"Our pursuit of justice will know no bounds," Nagarmal proclaimed, his tone steady and determined. Kishan conveyed silent agreement, fanning the inner flames of resolve. He pledged to transform Neelam's pain into a legacy. Taking a fortifying breath, he voiced his thoughts, rough with sorrow yet firm.

"You stand to me as a father," Kishan uttered sharply, his speech laced with bitter resentment. "And Neelam was akin to a daughter in my eyes. Now, I bear the weight of returning her spiritless form while you, our chieftain, deftly dodge your duty, clamouring still for an exchange—one lifeless vessel for another."

As emotions surged within Nagarmal, Kishan's voice became gentler, acknowledging their shared torment. "We were bested by a lunatic who prized power over his offspring. Your mourning now veils your wisdom! We cannot settle for anything less than revenge. No bartering."

To Kishan's surprise, Nagarmal took no umbrage at his fervent words. Indeed, there was a strange solace in knowing another soul bore the same anguish. Tears pooled in Kishan's eyes as he wept openly, standing vulnerable yet resolute, offering the only consolation he could muster.

With a swift motion, Kishan unsheathed his blade and thrust it towards the heavens. "By my family's honour, I pledge that as long as breath fills my lungs, King Balchand will be denied the solace of laying his son to rest," he declared, his voice resonating with unwavering resolve. "Our quest shall not cease until we claim your daughter's remains, perpetuating her curse to instil everlasting dread. The prince shall be refused the rites of a Hindu funeral, which might liberate his anguished soul. Our hands shall prevent any such ceremonies, ensuring Neelam's hex endures. Let her prophecy unfold. May their lineage crumble or exist eternally under the shadow of her curse."

After a tense silence, Nagarmal rose from his seat and held Kishan's trembling shoulder. "Kishan, you have been fiercely loyal all your life—your advice today carries great weight, even though it pains me to hear it," he said softly, his voice filled with admiration and sorrow.

Nagarmal paused, torn between his love for his daughter and his duty as their clan leader. He closed his eyes briefly as if searching for strength. When he opened them again, a steely determination shone through.

"No negotiation," he declared firmly. "We will retrieve my daughter's remains and the Prince's body as our own. Though it breaks my heart that they could not be united in this life, we must turn this tragedy into a legend that will strike fear into our enemies' hearts, particularly Balchand's family."

He paused once more, his mind racing for a plan. Suddenly, an idea struck him. "But here is what we shall do: instead of attacking the Bhatis head-on, we will infiltrate their dungeon and take back what is rightfully ours. And then, we will leave the Prince's body alongside my daughters in a defiant gesture to the king. Perhaps, one day, he may see the error of his ways."

Kishan looked at Nagarmal with respect as he spoke these bold words, but he also felt uneasy about this change in strategy. Nevertheless, he remained silent and nodded in agreement. "I will do as you ask," Kishan replied slowly before turning away, but something made him stop and turn back to face Nagarmal.

"Although we must retrieve her body, I want to leave a message behind for the Bhatis so that they understand the gravity of what has occurred here..." He gestured towards the blood-soaked bandages wrapped around Nagarmal's hands. "Give me those severed fingers - let King Balchand see how vengeful you are. We will leave the Prince's body in place of Neelam's and bring her back. That fool Balchand will never think of looking for the Prince's body in the crypt where he thinks he buried Neelam alive."

The scene was tense as Kishan stood before the Banjara chief, his expression conveying a sense of urgency and gravity. His furrowed brow accentuated his earnest appeal as he fervently prayed to the tribal leader to procure the very dagger that the Prince had used to wound himself fatally. After the initial shock, the chief agreed and promptly summoned his physician. Soon, a bundle stained with blood and three severed fingers was handed over to Kishan, sending a chill down his spine as he reluctantly accepted the grim token. With steely resolve, Kishan rallied his faithful warriors under the cover of night and set out on their mission.

Shrouded in darkness, they discovered the hidden remains of the prince. They carefully loaded them onto a horse, carrying the weight of sorrow and loyalty as they embarked towards Chief Balchand's estate. The palace loomed eerily in the dark, its imposing spires casting ghostly silhouettes under the night sky. The air was heavy with mournful cries and the pungent aroma of incense, adding an otherworldly feel to the atmosphere.

Their hearts pounding, they dismounted and disguised themselves in stolen uniforms of Balchand's guard, moving stealthily with measured, deliberate footsteps towards a side door to the courtyard. Each step felt like an eternity as Kishan led them towards the dungeon door, his grip on his sword turning his knuckles ashen. The tension was palpable as they worked to breach the bricks surrounding Neelam's tomb, every strike of their tools fuelling Kishan's frustration.

Finally, after what seemed like an eternity, they created enough space to see Neelam's lifeless body hanging from chains on the wall. A surge of fury ignited within Kishan as he let out a primal roar, determined to reach her despite feeling helpless at the turn of events. With trembling hands, they tenderly released her from the shackles, shrouding her gently in cloth.

They grieved over their cherished Prince and then reverently laid remains to rest in a secret alcove. They laid the dagger by his side and a small chest containing Nagamal's three severed digits as a cryptic signpost for those who might, one day, unravel this enigma.Using simple tools of lime and clay from the earth, they laboriously sealed the tomb, their clothes adorned with the dust of their solemn task.

Carrying Neelam's earthly remains with utmost respect, they emerged through the humble servants' passage, the weight of their mission etched on their determined faces.

Despite his fatigue, Kishan's eyes still burned with determination as he placed Neelam's lifeless body on the fourth empty horse.As he adjusted it into place, Neelam's mutilated foot was revealed. Kishan pushed it back into the concealing, protective blanket with trembling hands. His touch remained gentle as if Neelam was deep asleep. A lump rose in Kishan's throat. Suddenly, a mad tinge of red overcame him.

He held his sword scabbard and moaned in frustration. "I must go back inside and slit the throat of both King Balchand and his wife for this!"

His companions quickly hushed him, knowing rash actions could endanger them all. After calming himself, Kishan mounted his horse and began the ojourney back to the to the Banjara village.

The journey was long but steady, with each step a rhythmic procession towards their home.

As dawn began to break over the horizon, Kishan and the village priest arrived at their destination. They exchanged sombre words before making their way to Nagarmal's house. The family received their deceased daughter without uttering a single word, their fear of King Balchand keeping them quiet. More than sorrow, an uneasy tension gripped everyone in the village.

Kishan and Nagarmal quietly left with Neelam's corpse to the Banjara temple to seek guidance from the priest on how best to conceal Neelam's corpse so that it would never be found, leaving the two souls in abeyance and allow the curse to carry its course.

The silent procession of the three horses moved slowly in the direction of the temple.

They reached the temple, where the priest approached them with arms raised in silent welcome. Nagarmal, who had been at the front, raised his hand in greeting to the priest but suddenly slumped in his saddle and groaned, "I am done."

As his horse sensed something amiss, it whined and jostled nervously. Suddenly, Nagarmal fell forward like a limp grain bag, tumbling off the back of the horse with a heavy thud. Kishan, filled with concern, rushed to Nagarmal's side and knelt beside him, cradling his Chief 's now still head. A chilling realisation set in as he saw his chief 's vacant stare, his eyes fixed on the endless void. At that moment, Kishan knew that Nagarmal had succumbed to the consuming grief that had been gnawing at him since the loss of his daughter. Emotions streamed down Kishan's face as he bowed his head and whispered a heartfelt prayer for his departed chief.

Kishan turned towards the priest, his eyes filled with tears. "Father, why is fate so cruel?" The priest's compassionate gaze met his, offering a silent understanding that words could not convey. The priest stepped closer and shook Kishan by his shoulders to jolt him back to reality. In his firm grip, Kishan found a semblance of stability amidst the chaos. They now had to consider two funerals.

Kishan and the priest trudged with the horses back to the Banjara temple. The priest remained silent, lost in thought, as Kishan followed obediently. When they reached the palace's central courtyard, the priest turned to Kishan with a solemn look on his face.

"If we cremate her and perform the last rites, then her soul will be free. But if King Balchand also finds the prince's body and cremates him, then both souls will be released, and Neelam's curse will be lifted. The guilty will never be punished," he said as he touched Kishan's shoulder.

Nearby, the priest, standing solemnly, offered a silent benediction for Nagarmal's soul.

A resounding echo of emptiness engulfed Kishan amid a sombre gathering. Experiencing the simultaneous departure of his companion and the cherished Neelam plunged him into a well of sorrow and isolation.

Observing the priest tend to Nagarmal's remains for the last rites only intensified the surreal sense of detachment within him.

From afar, Kishan's gaze lingered as the priest meticulously removed all signs of royalty, including the turban, a stark reminder that they would grace Nagarmal no longer.

As dusk descended, the pyre was set ablaze, the flames reaching for the heavens in a dance shroudedin smoke. In respectful silence, Kishan and the priest bore witness to Nagarmal's earthly vessel's surrender to the fire, a final act of closure. The erratic light of the fire painted eerie visages upon their countenances, mirroring the cruel finality of their grief. Kishan's eyes brimmed with grief, yet he fortified his resolve, withholding the tears, standing undaunted by the weight of loss for Nagarmal, Neelam, and himself.

Once the embers were cold and the fire was gone, the priest and Kishan resumed their travels. As per custom, they planned to collect Nagarmal's ashes at daybreak on the third day. But first, they had to carry out another responsibility—locating a hidden spot, known only to them, to lay Neelam to rest.

Chapter 17:

Underwater but Dry

"To live in hearts we leave behind is not to die."

– Thomas Campbell

Kishan and the priest carefully wove their way through the bustling streets of Jodhpur, their movements purposeful and almost furtive as they concealed Neelam's lifeless body with a hastily arranged bale of cotton. Amidst the din of merchants and customers, they navigated the crowded thoroughfares, their steps blending seamlessly with the city's vibrant energy.

They sought refuge from the harsh daylight by skilfully slipping into the comforting shadows, where they appeared to disappear into the maze of twisting alleyways and bustling markets. After a long and careful journey, they finally reached a secluded house nestled within the protective embrace of the city walls. Kishan's sister, Saraswati, welcomed them with warm hospitality, but her welcoming expression quickly turned to concern when she saw the distress on Kishan's face. She urgently called for her husband, Umaid Singh, who was known for his sharp intellect and expertise in managing Jodhpur's reservoirs.

As they anxiously awaited Umaid's arrival, Kishan and the priest were momentarily suspended in tense silence. Their eyes were unwaveringly fixed on every movement in anticipation. When he finally entered the room, they wasted no time in urgently recounting the tragic turn of events that had led them there. Their voices were weighted with the burden of bearing Neelam's lifeless form. Umaid listened intently, the reflection in his eyes conveying a potent blend of steely determination and an unyielding thirst for retribution.

Over a leisurely cup of tea, Umaid unfurled a map that adorned the wall, his eyes twinkling with anticipation. He eagerly recounted to Kishan the existence of an elaborate underground maze known as 'Tapi Bawri', employed for conserving water. With enthusiasm, he spoke of this year's harsh drought toll and sketched out their blueprint for adventure at this arcane site. "This year's drought has left our water levels at their lowest in fifty years," he continued grimly.

Umaid animatedly discussed the reservoir's complex architecture, historical value, and the intent behind its creation. It represented not merely a lifeline for water but a monument to ancient architects' cultural essence and ingenuity. Adorned with graceful pillars, archways, sculptures, and murals, it exuded tranquillity. He narrated the extensive network of passageways designed ingeniously to mitigate flooding, mentioning how this year's lowered water levels proved advantageous.

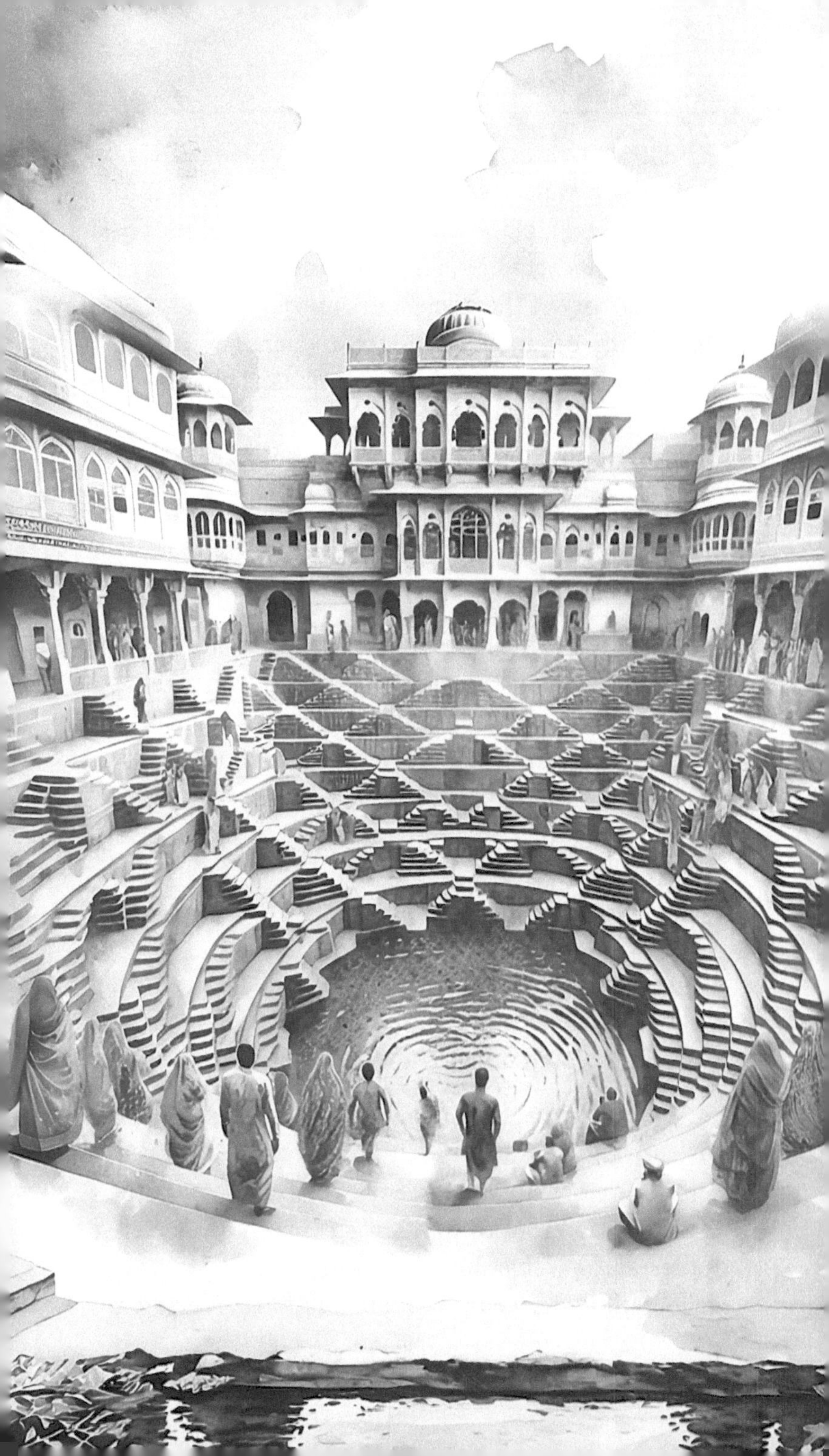

The Bawri, as the reservoir was called, was more than just a water source. It was a symbol of culture and heritage, a place where people gathered for social and religious activities, and a testament to the wisdom and creativity of the ancient architects. The steps were lined with ornamental pillars and arches decorated with intricate carvings and paintings. The chambers were adorned with sculptures, creating a serene and soothing ambience.

The Bawri was a marvel of beauty and functionality, a lifeline for the region's people to store drinkable, potable water.

The network of sloping tunnels was an intricate maze designed to prevent flooding. Even when the water rose, it would not submerge all the chambers, leaving only limited access underwater.

The caretaker enthusiastically gestured and explained that the water level had receded to the fourth level this year, a fortunate circumstance for their plans.

It meant they could take the body four stories down and use one of the tunnels to reach a dry pocket where they could hide it.

They stood at a critical juncture in their mission, fuelled by meticulous strategy and imaginative solutions. Seeking justice for Neelam's untimely demise was now within reach in these secretive subterranean chambers. Precision and thorough deliberation marked their preparations, bracing for what would unfold under the twilight shroud, driven by vindication for their cherished Neelam.

Kishan and the priest surveyed their surroundings with a shared understanding and knowing glances. They had chosen this secluded location, hidden from prying eyes and filled with potential for their nefarious plans. Neelam's body would be concealed here, forever lost to the world. With Umaid as their guide, they were confident in their ability to finally exact revenge on those responsible for her premature death.

Beneath a veiled night sky, the trio made their way, burdened with the sad weight of Neelam's departed spirit, their lanterns slicing through the obscurity with soft, haunting illumination. Arriving at Tapi Bawri, an unassuming edifice intertwined with wild greenery, they observed the shadowy waters at its heart dance under the quivering lamplight. The water lilies and green algae bathed in an otherworldly luminescence upon the darkened liquid expanse.

Starting from the sixth level of the structure, just above ground level, they cautiously made their way down to the fourth level, where they spotted an alcove with steps leading into a dark passage that sloped steeply upwards. With trepidation tickling their nerves, they forged ahead into the moist passage, its atmosphere thick with the scent of decaying fungi. Wading through knee-deep waters, they emerged into a room adorned with relics of timeworn wood and a crude stone tabletop. The keeper, trailing just behind and setting his lamp upon that worn table, let out a soft chuckle. Mopping his brow from the cloying heat, he remarked on their courage for delving so deep into Tapi Bawri's heart—a place long avoided by locals who whispered frightful stories of malevolent phantoms that lingered in its shadows.

Umaid pointed to a raised stone slab in the chamber and declared it Neelam's final resting place.

Kishan and the priest carefully laid her down on the cold stone slab before sitting down to catch their breath. In a sudden burst of movement, Kishan lunged forward and pressed a dagger against the caretaker's throat, causing him to give a knowing but amused grin. The caretaker spoke calmly, choosing his words with care. "I understand that speaking of this secret is forbidden. You can trust me; if you wish, I will return to my family in Bikaner and start farming. Your sister need not become a widow tonight."

Speaking in a reconciliatory tone, the priest implored Kishan to spare the caretaker's life. Kishan nodded at the priest's urging and felt relieved for his sister.

"Kishan, he doesn't deserve to die. I believe we can trust him with this secret. And when we are ready, we will return to move Neelam's body elsewhere."

Kishan seemed unsure as he pulled away his knife from the caretaker's throat, even though he was his own sister's husband. He fumbled through his tunic and took out a small bag, throwing it towards the caretaker.

"This is for your silence," Kishan threatened. The caretaker opened the bag and found gold coins stuffed inside. There was more than enough money to ensure not only his silence but that of his future generations.

"We must leave right now," Kishan urged the other two to retrace their steps.

The trio navigated darkness. Their footsteps were heavy against the stone steps leading up to the fourth level. The only light source was a flickering lantern, casting eerie shadows along the ancient walls. As they climbed two more levels, their lungs strained for air, and their legs burned with exhaustion. Finally reaching the top, they emerged from the Bawdi and were met with a gust of cool night air. The caretaker silently gathered his few belongings and prepared to leave.

As they raced towards Kishan's sister's residence, Kishan and the priest wasted no time. Frantic and determined, they quickly gathered their horses and rode off without saying goodbye—their destination: the bank of the lake, where Nagarmal's funeral pyre had been set ablaze.

When they arrived, they frantically sifted through the ashes for any remains. Each charred fragment they found was carefully collected and placed into an urn: a tooth here, a bone there.

With heavy hearts, Kishan and the priest silently returned to their village. As they unloaded the urn at Nagarmal's house, chaos erupted throughout the Banjara village. Word spread like wildfire of Chief Nagarmal's passing and the shocking disappearance of Neelam's mortal remains.

Chapter 18:

She Lies in Peace

"Death is a natural part of life. Rejoice for those around you who transform into the Force. Mourn them, do not. Miss them, do not."

– Star Wars: Revenge of the Sith

With a rub of his hands and a spark in his eyes, Andrew was the picture of excitement, but it wasn't long before a shadow of doubt dimmed his glow. A shiver of apprehension overtook the thrill.

"Remains of the corpse intact? Oh, who am I kidding? After 300 years, it is probably nothing but dust," he conjectured, his query floating out into the tense silence. A palpable charge hung thick amongst the group, a concoction of eagerness and anxiety as they combined their strategy. Upon their return to the Gladwell abode, an anxious Sandhya awaited, bursting at the seams for news of the eventful period she missed. Candice deftly filled the gaps, rekindling a fire of optimism within Sandhya. Longing to be part of the quest to uncover Neelam's remains, Sandhya beseeched Andrew. Yet, with steadfast resolve, he denied her plea, invoking the peril that Tapi Bawri posed.

Meanwhile, Commissioner Prabhat reached out to Baba Kanmal in a frantic appeal for assistance with the search. Amid their discussions, Shyam interrupted with news that someone was requesting an audience with them. A weathered Banjara elder, adorned in worn, vibrant garments embellished with beads and feathers, entered wordlessly. In a cryptic gesture, the elder passed Andrew a small metal cylinder containing a parchment map left behind by his ancestor, Kishan.

Despite the initial difficulty opening it, Shyam came to the rescue with a small saw, allowing them to pry open the impenetrable metal cap carefully. Inside, Andrew discovered a weathered parchment tightly wound with a string. He unfurled the parchment with practice, revealing faint charcoal depictions of the Bawri, an ancient stepwell steeped in legend and curses. A circle in one corner of the parchment was inscribed with a single word in Hindi: "Daughter."

Andrew's finger tapped eagerly on the paper as he exclaimed, "I believe this is about Neelam!"

His companions all nodded in determined agreement.

In a flurry, Andrew urgently contacted Commissioner Prabhat, letting him know that they had the Prince's remains and that members of the Bhati clan were converging in Jodhpur to pay their respects with a dignified funeral—which had been wrongfully withheld from the departed prince.

With passion weaving through her words, Candice announced, "Neelam must be our next stop, quickly. If we could, orchestrating concurrent memorial services would be ideal."

Before they arrived in Jodhpur, Candice had already briefed Vaibhav Bhati on the unfolding events. His diplomatic efforts to elicit aid from the influential Rathore royal lineage, stewards of the area since the 1400s, were met with success, much to their relief.

Come dawn, Commissioner Prabhat showed up in an official vehicle to collect Candice, Andrew, and Sandhya. They traversed the city's historic district until reaching a part where the roads were too snug for their truck to continue. Stepping onto the street brimming with confusion, Sandhya questioned, "Is this our destination?"

The Commissioner offered a gentle laugh and replied, "Not quite. Here, we switch to an auto-rickshaw for the rest of the trek; these alleys are a squeeze for anything larger." He pointed ahead while calmingly saying, "Fear not. We'll venture as near to Tapi Bawri as we can."

Advancing boldly down the busy thoroughfare, their group caught the eye of a roaming rickshaw, its black-and-yellow facade stark against the bustling backdrop. Its driver expertly gunned the engine, skillfully navigating slimmer lanes until veering down a passageway so tight that it seemed tailor-made for their rickshaw alone, adding an electrifying sense of intrigue to their journey.

They found themselves in a charming little square, hidden off the meandering path by some fate. The

Commissioner's boots echoed on the ancient stones as they left their vehicles behind. They trod a short distance until a sharp turn revealed an imposing structure clawing towards the sky with its grey walls. Adorned in crisp military regalia, the men at the entrance stood ramrod straight and saluted their senior's arrival. Beckoning for the site's caretaker and delegates, the group entered an opulent hall brimming with unease.

A man, capped in authority, sprang up, his voice charged with urgency as he spotted the Commissioner. "Why are we gathered here, Commissioner Prabhat? Civilian access is barred! What urgent matter brings us this disruption?"

Cue the barrage of inquiries from the others. Commissioner Prabhat cast a sobering gaze over the lot and gestured for silence. "Gentlefolk," he commanded attention, "remain composed and hear me out."

Stepping into the limelight, he narrated the purpose behind Andrew and Candice's visit. A wave of suspicion washed over the collective visages, a tangible mistrust hanging heavy as he relayed his narrative. The sceptical man in the cap pierced the air with incredulity. "What assurances do we have that you aren't scavenging for riches? Can such tales be believed?"

His scepticism resonated through the room, reflected by nods and murmurs of validation. Yet, the Commissioner proffered a straightforward proposal.

"Witness our every move. Accompany, walk to the chamber, and observe firsthand—no lore or treasure shall remain concealed."

An onlooker snorted contempt at this suggestion, while another smirked haughtily in reply: "Walk with us? Walk on water, you mean! The Bawri is full to the brim. How do you propose to get across?" The Commissioner's expression remained calm as he offered a solution, his voice carrying authority and conviction.

Shadowed by Candice's vigilant gaze, Andrew swiftly converted the engineer's language into something understandable as they threaded their way in the wake of the cap-donned leader. Navigating a corridor with scarce light, a pair of elderly women observed them, eyes brimming with fascination. They concluded their trek at the brink of a water body, deceptively narrow at forty feet across, yet seemingly infinite in its lengthwise stretch—a mirror still and untouched.

The engineer danced his finger atop the map, caressing the topography of the Bawri as though he were feeling the pulse of its storied walls under his skin. Abruptly halting, he anchored his finger on the sixth level illustrated within the map's confines. "Something is not right here," he growled, his eyes narrow and intense.

Andrew stationed himself before a pair of grand maps sprawled across a table pieced together in haste. Hours had slipped by, but the enigma within the cartographic lines still eluded him. The first chart showcased the age-worn outlines of the tower wrapped around the Bawri, while its companion illustrated recent architectural additions. As Andrew delved deeper into the comparison, the anomalies stood out starkly. The fourth-floor level plunged into a watery abyss for no less than twenty feet, a depth unreachable by simple tunnelling methods. His pulse quickened at the realisation: veiled chambers should lie within reach from this drowned floor, hidden entirely behind a veil of aqueous mystery. It was as if a swath of the palace had vanished from human eyes. With mounting disbelief, Andrew absorbed the astonishing oversight—the self-professed palace expert engineer had glossed over a vital facet. Puzzled yet resolute, Andrew coupled his consternation with action, resting elbows on the maps as he scavenged through them for clues.

With tenacity anchoring his spirit, inspiration sparked like flint to tinder in Andrew's thoughts, prompting him to seize a pencil and begin a frenzied dance of sketching upon the second map. The swift strokes of his vision gave birth to an 'Underwater Tunnel'—the letters stamped with conviction, surrounded by meticulous notes of the smaller script. A path to the concealed chamber emerged in his mind's eye and, with it, a gateway to answers.

A sigh of solace enveloped Andrew, soothing his weary soul as the flicker of understanding kindled.

The riddle of hours seemed to unravel before him, promising that the elusive truth lingered just within arm's reach. He flipped fervently between the charts, fervour morphing swiftly to foreboding.

Despair gripped Andrew's heart, dragging him to the ground as he peered through a haze of urgency at the maps. A chilling realisation dawned on him—to navigate these submerged shadows, they needed to master the underwater domain. The impulse to secure diving gear was overwhelming, for the quest could only continue with such preparation.

Gathering his wits, he looked up at the Commissioner and asked in a strained voice, "Have you managed to find trained divers for this job?" Their role was crucial to his plan; his efforts would only be worthwhile with them.

Without hesitation, the Commissioner pointed to two figures nearby and ordered them to step forward. After briefly assessing their skills, the men retrieved their gear and prepared to dive. Andrew and Candice couldn't help but notice that their equipment seemed ancient and outdated, relics from a bygone era. The Commissioner eyed the gear sceptically, but the men's confident expressions betrayed no fear or doubt. Their unwavering bravery was palpable, inspiring awe in the onlookers and a deep sense of inspiration.

Commissioner Prabhat's observations of Andrew and Candice's troubled visages, carved with lines of anxiety, were apparent. He delivered the stark reality with a voice that carried the weight of the situation: "This stark expanse is all we have amidst the sands. Anticipate nothing more." His words hung heavy in the air, underscoring the gravity of their mission.

With trepidation coiling within him, Andrew mustered an encouraging grin for Candice, vowing with unwavering determination, "Fear not. I shall venture below with our colleagues to survey the conditions. Should safety permit, you'll be my next priority." His resolve was palpable, cutting through the tension like a beacon of hope. Nonetheless, Candice's face was a canvas of reluctance, her gaze reflecting an unsettled spirit. The enigma entwining their quest lay dense in the atmosphere, infusing their escapade with an electrifying sense of suspense.

Resolved to dispel her apprehensions, Andrew proposed to the Commissioner, "Our inventory must expand to include additional diving apparatus, ensuring Candice can accompany the plunge into mystery." At his words, anticipation sparked in Candice's eyes, not from dread but from the intoxicating allure of inching closer to unravelling their enigmatic charge.

With all protocols in place, Andrew and his compatriot donned their underwater armoury, ready to brave the subaqueous corridors of the Bawri. As they submerged beyond the realm of warmth, each inhalation became a feat, growing sharper and fraught with difficulty. The water's cold crept like a shadow across their forms, compelling a steely resolve from

Andrew. These trials wove another tense thread into the fabric of their pursuit.

As Andrew secured his mask and tweaked the torch beam, relief coursed through him, for the light cut through the abyss, serving as a herald through the gloom. Yet, an undercurrent of disquiet clung to him tenaciously as they delved deeper into the Bawri's secrets shrouded beneath.

When they reached the fourth floor, an unexpected obstacle caught them off guard – a once-open tunnel now blocked by an impenetrable brick wall. Scanning the barrier with his light, Andrew could find no cracks or hints of passage. With a sense of bewilderment tugging at them, he gestured to his companion to take an alternative route, venturing into the shrouded territories ahead. This unforeseen hurdle threw them for a loop, much like a dramatic plot twist in a suspenseful tale, deepening the mystery of their journey.

Further into the abyss, amidst the shadows and silt, Andrew spotted a subtle hint of lustre that marked a concealed entrance—evidence of a passage time had veiled from memory. This secret corridor appeared as if it rose from the very fabric of the water itself, ushering them onward to an area they might have missed had the way not been barred earlier.

Trailing through liquid corridors encased by ghostly walls, they followed this newly revealed path until it narrowed to a mere fissure leading to a barely visible passageway. Anxiety whispered through Andrew's mind, "Could this be the gateway?" Despite their hopes, the new chamber yielded no secrets. It dawned on them that the only way forward was to breach the stubborn masonry before them to confirm if another room awaited in silent vigil.

Meanwhile, Candice remained above the surface, her spirit blending excitement and trepidation. She felt every second stretch on, her unease growing. After what seemed like an age, salvation bubbled from the depths at the far edge of the pool. A shoal of bubbles heralded the divers' return, washing away her anxiety like whispers unto water; the explorers had resurfaced.

Rescued from the aquatic depths, Commissioner Prabhat swiftly briefed Andrew alongside Sandhya. His mission was to wield a pickaxe in the watery abyss, targeting bricks to dismantle an underwater barrier.

In a flurry of activity, extra diving equipment was acquired, paired with two sharp-edged pickaxes and four sturdy metal rods to act as makeshift expansion bolts. Plunging back beneath the waves, Andrew and his fellow divers set upon the brickwork with their tools. Their progress, although incremental, was unwavering; they pried away enough bricks for the expansion bolts to take hold. The bolts, secured and roped, awaited their above-water cue to initiate the collapse of the submerged wall. Their determination was a beacon of inspiration, a testament to the power of human resilience in the face of adversity.

Once back on the surface, they presented the ropes – now linked with the expansion bolts – to Commissioner Prabhat. A coordinated team took charge, allowing slack before rapidly retreating, harnessing pull and momentum to wrench more bricks from the unseen wall below. It was a testament to raw persistence and muscle sans the leverage of machinery or electric assistance. Their unity was palpable, each member contributing strength and skill to the collective effort, fostering a deep camaraderie.

With each robust tug, they unseated further bricks. With every heave, renewed vigour pulsed through the group, ultimately yanking all four bolts loose as the bricks cascaded downward.

Elation propelled Andrew. He re-entered the water with a fellow diver, eager to witness their labour's victory over the wall. They sped downwards, their hearts filled with the sweet taste of triumph, a reward for their unwavering determination and relentless effort.

By chance, their gaze fell upon an audacious break in the once-pristine wall of bricks. With renewed vigour, they ventured through the rift, ascending the gentle incline until they emerged into a slowly tapering corridor. Their pulses quickened as they climbed to an archaic hall, its grandeur marred by the patina of age.

Yet, when Andrew lifted his mask to appreciate the vista better, he was startled by the scant oxygen that greeted him. He hastily secured his mask again and pursued his partner through the chamber's deeper realms. An eerie silence enveloped them, augmenting the air of enigma and awe.

They spotted an unusual relic on a stone altar at the end of the room, covered with thick burlap cloth. Driven by an insatiable thirst for knowledge, they approached with great anticipation. As they prepared to examine the mystery before them with caution, the dim light from their torches cast strange shadows over the worn-out chamber.

Andrew's heart raced as they uncovered the disturbing relic of the past – a skeleton with grim tales reflected in its shattered ankle bone. But before his partner could touch the relic, Andrew gestured emphatically at the ankle that dangled at an unnatural angle, revealing the broken bone and urging them to retreat quickly. They retraced their steps through the passage and emerged back into daylight. Gasping for air, Andrew's excited shout broke the silence, his arms flailing to convey the significance of their discovery.

"We've got her! She's down there!" he shouted. A helpful hand reached out to haul him ashore. As he regained composure and crouched on solid ground, he eagerly shared the revelation.

"She's right where we hoped she'd be," Andrew said. Turning to Candice, who absorbed every word with captivated focus, he urged, "We require some kind of watertight covering—vinyl tarps, perhaps—to bundle her up for the ascent."

Candice, stubborn as ever, with a spark of fascination in her eyes, determinedly stated, "I must witness her retrieval myself. I need to see it firsthand."

Andrew knew she would not budge despite his reservations unless he allowed her to come along. He could sense her unwavering determination and knew it would only cause problems if he denied her request.

The Commissioner requested provisions and soon armed the group with sturdy polyethene sacks to transport the deceased to a morgue. Galvanised by determination, Andrew, Candice, and two experienced divers joined forces to escort Neelam through the murky waters to safety. The journey was treacherous, but they were determined to bring their discovery back to the surface. Despite feeling exhausted and physically taxed, Andrew and Candice pressed on with unwavering determination, knowing what awaited them would make every struggle worthwhile.

The two trained divers led the way, Candice and Andrew making up the rear to support each other, but their pace was slower than the other two. They had to navigate through a labyrinth of submerged tunnels, avoiding sharp rocks and debris that threatened to cut their skin or damage their equipment.

The water was murky and cold, reducing their visibility and numbing their senses. They could only rely on their flashlights and instincts to guide them through the dark and hostile environment.

From the water's depths into the hidden corridor, Andrew's light revealed a stone table upon which a decaying skeleton adorned with tattered clothing lay. With a pounding heart filled with hope, Candice cautiously approached the remains. The corridor was narrow and damp, with walls covered in moss and algae. The air was stale and musty, as if no one had breathed it for centuries. The only sound was water dripping from the ceiling, creating a rhythmic and eerie echo. Candice felt a chill run down her spine as she reached the end of the corridor and entered the chamber. It was a small and circular room with a domed ceiling and no light coming in except for the flashlights brought down by the divers. The chamber was bare except for the raised stone table and the skeleton. It looked like a tomb, a place of final resting for the lost and forgotten.

It was not until Andrew directed his light towards the foot of the skeleton that Candice gasped in shock. It lay shattered and dangling at an awkward angle, evidence of the brutal fate that had befallen Neelam.

Candice felt a surge of emotion as she realised that this woman had suffered immense sorrow. She felt a mix of awe, admiration, sadness, and anger. She wondered what Neelam had gone through and what she had seen, heard, and felt.

Under the weight of their duty and the sorrow in their hearts, they delicately wrapped Neelam's remains in the body bag. They commenced their strenuous journey back to the surface, displaying unwavering dedication to their mission.

The murky waters churned violently, frothing and foaming as if alive with their energy. The crowd watched with anticipation and relief, their eyes glued to the surface where something weighty and precious was about to emerge. Hands reached out frantically, fingers grasping for purchase on the body bag containing Neelam's remains. Each person seemed afraid it would slip away into the depths again.

Candice emerged from the water, her trembling body dripping with exhaustion and grief. She could barely stand independently but was supported by careful hands that guided her onto dry land. Her diving suit clung to her skin like a second layer, heavy with moisture and weighing her down.

The atmosphere was thick with emotion as Sandhya stood waiting for her friend, offering silent solace in the face of their shared tragedy. Their weary steps were a testament to this journey's toll. Every step felt like wading through molasses, each breath a struggle against the weight of their sorrow.

And then, as if to emphasise the gravity of this moment, the skies suddenly parted, and a soft rain began to fall from above. The cool droplets cleansed and purified everything in their path, washing away grime and dirt and infusing the air with a sense of renewal and hope. The sound of rain hitting the ground created a soothing melody, providing a much-needed respite from the intense emotions swirling around them.

Under the sheltering sky, the assembly stood united in profound catharsis. It was as if the rain symbolised a fresh start and a promising future, washing away all past pain and hurt. Even Commissioner Prabhat, who had stoically observed nearby, was moved to break the heavy stillness in the air. His eyes widened in awe at the picturesque sky above, adorned with vibrant red and orange hues as the sun descended, casting a warm, golden glow over everything below. "It seems like even the gods themselves are celebrating today," he mused aloud, his voice filled with wonder.

Amidst all this beauty and serenity, Candice felt an overwhelming sense of release and healing. The gentle breeze caressed her skin, carrying away all traces of pain and sorrow. The expanse of blue above seemed limitless, igniting within her a feeling of boundless opportunity. It was as if the rain had washed away all her doubts and fears, leaving only hope and possibility behind.

As she turned to look at Andrew, their eyes met in a profound connection, a reflection of the transformative power of this moment. Standing side by side, they basked in the tranquil beauty surrounding them, cherishing its significance. Sandhya approached them and stood snugly between them, interlocking hands with Candice and Andrew in a comforting embrace, symbolising their victory and unity.

With the descent of the sun, everything fell into place for Candice. All her struggles, pain, and heartache suddenly made sense. It was like taking a leap of faith and being rewarded with an unexpected blessing. As she gazed at the sky above, she couldn't help but feel grateful for the rain that had brought such profound change and renewal to her life. She closed her eyes and let the rain wash over her face, feeling a sense of peace and wholeness that she hadn't felt in a long time.

Chapter 19:

Death is But a Condition

"As the different streams having their sources in different places all mingle their water in the sea, so, O Lord, the different paths which men take through different tendencies, various though they appear, crooked or straight, all lead to thee."

– Swami Vivekananda's speech at the World Parliament of Religions, Chicago, 11 Sept 1893.

The chill of the air was unyielding, pressing down upon the crowd that had gathered in shared sorrow. They were there to say their final goodbyes to Prince Bhanwar and Neelam. The cold was biting, yet the heavy mantle of grief cloaked the assembly, muting all but their collective heartache as they paid tribute to the star-crossed pair whose lives ceased too early, plunging everyone into deep lament.

Amid those assembled stood Candice, adorned in the traditional garb of a Hindu mourner, her presence an exception granted in honour of the event she now attended. Tears carved tracks on her cheeks, mirroring the poignant scenes that played out before her, a sharp contrast to the life decisions about corporate bonds she faced just weeks prior.

Overlooking the two shrouded figures perched on a fragrant sandalwood pyre, destined for liberation by fire as prescribed by ancient scriptures, she felt the weight of sorrow anchoring her spirit.

Baba Kanmal, accompanied by villagers from Banjara, was observed with solemn respect, honouring Neelam's journey to eternity. Even Vaibhav Bhati found his way among the mourners, a familiar solace in the sea of grieving faces.

As the priests intoned sacred verses and purifying rites, seeking equilibrium in a karmic cycle jolted by Prince Bhanwar's sorrowful demise, time seemed to pause respectfully, paying homage to the departed souls.

Andrew spellbound Candice as he unfolded the profound meaning of cremation. Her eyes brimmed with inquiry and bewilderment, yet his reassuring touch eased her turmoil. He murmured with a strength that belied his gentleness, "The physical form is but a shell for the spirit. It doesn't truly vanish; it transitions beyond our mundane realm. These flames are symbolic; they release and sanctify the soul from its bodily chains. Bear in mind that we revert to ashes. To dust, we return!"

Baba Kanmal, embodying resolute reverence, advanced carrying a torch destined to ignite the pyres for Neelam and the Prince, with Vaibhav treading respectfully behind. In the reverent hush, Candice observed the poignant tableau unfolding before her. Shrouded in death's embrace, Neelam and Bhanwar rested atop a fragrant edifice of sandalwood, poised for the purifying inferno of their last rites.

The subdued air bore the rich fragrance of sandalwood, while marigold garlands cast a soft glow over the hallowed ground, injecting bursts of life into the grave ritual. As Hindu customs sought to liberate their terrene souls, sorrow and longing surged within her.

While the priest chanted sacred verses, Candice grappled with a farewell to two souls she'd learned in spirit through recent happenings.

The pyre's smoke billowed, cloaking Neelam and Bhanwar's mortal shapes. Candice could feel the warmth on her skin and the saccharine aroma of the sandalwood as it charred. Through the cloud of tears blurring her vision, she listened to the tranquil narrative of the unending spirit embarking on its definitive odyssey. Amidst the grief, these sacred observations brought Candice a measure of peace.

As the inferno blazed with unyielding intensity, they retreated, and eventually, all tangible remnants of what had been once now being consumed by the fire. A heavy hush fell over them as they carried out the final rites, each moment saturated with an acute awareness of loss yet paradoxically marked by the silent tick of time pausing in deference to their sorrow.

In this heart of despair, surprisingly, tiny flickers of hope and rebirth began to emerge within them.

Candice paused, the tender kiss of the fire's glow against her skin allowing a moment of catharsis, embracing the looming horizon of new beginnings. Though forever halting their earthly journey, the tragic union of Prince Bhanwar and Neelam spoke of a love so deep that it carved its echoes into the infinite.

The ceremony ended with solemn tributes as each mourner dissolved into the thickening night. Only the soft glow of dying embers witnessed the young spirits' passage, symbolising undiminished presences and a bond sealed by eternal affection.

When they gathered again after three days to tend to their legacy, a quilt of emotions swathed Candice as she sifted through the warm powder of memories past. Every handful was a poignant emblem of pure love, severed untimely by destiny's harsh snare.

Her gaze lifted to find a Hindu priest nearby, his presence a serene port in the storm of their grief. He drew closer, offering words in a compassionate murmur.

"My child, your sorrow is not unseen, but understand that our ancestors have paved these steps for us. We return on the third day to claim the ashes, following the belief that it takes this time for the soul to emancipate from the flesh, ascending to ancestral realms. Gathering their remnants is not merely a formality; it is an act of homage — a guiding light to serenity for their spirits, and a silent thanksgiving for the life they lived, for the love they endowed upon us."

In the depths of mourning, a ray of hope pierced through the potential for mending and growth in the wake of catastrophe. Seeing distress on Candice's face, the priest led her to a corner of the rooftop where he bade her sit on the edge with the city of Jodhpur below her and the lofty towers of Mehrangarh Fort. Candice breathed in the fresh air and felt comforted. The priest started talking to her in a calm voice.

Candice listened carefully to his caring words. Her curiosity finally got the better of her. "Sir, I noticed that Hindu funerals are quite different from what I am used to," she began, her eyes reflecting her curiosity. "Could you explain the importance of these rituals?"

With a gentle smile, the priest responded, "In Hinduism, death is not seen as the end, but a transition. Our rituals help the departed soul journey to the next life. We believe in reincarnation, and these rites are a way to ensure a peaceful transition."

Candice nodded, taking in his words. "That's a comforting thought. But why is there so much sadness, and yet so much happiness at the same time?"

"Life, Candice, is a mix of joy and sorrow," the priest explained. "We mourn the loss of a loved one, but we also celebrate their life and the journey they are about to embark on. It's a bittersweet moment."

"But how does one cope with so much pain and suffering?" Candice asked, her voice barely above

a whisper, as she suddenly thought of Chris and Jadene—a lump formed in her throat.

"Hindu philosophy teaches us that pain and suffering are part of life, just as joy and happiness are. They are two sides of the same coin. We learn to accept both with grace. It's through experiencing these highs and lows that we grow and evolve as individuals," the priest shared, his voice filled with wisdom.

Candice paused, absorbing his words before asking her next question. "But what happens to the soul after it departs from the earth?"

"We believe that the soul embarks on a journey to another realm, guided by the rituals performed during the funeral. The soul goes through various stages, eventually reaching a state of peace and preparing for the next life," the priest explained.

"And how will we know whether our loved ones have found peace at the other end?" Candice asked, her voice laced with longing.

"We may not have a definitive answer, my child. But our faith and the rituals we perform give us comfort, believing that we have done our part to aid their journey. The peace we seek is often within ourselves, in accepting the cycle of life and death and cherishing the memories of our loved ones," the priest concluded, his words resonating with a profound truth.

The priest then raised his palm and asked her to look around.

"Look below you and around you. What do you see? You see a city on the move. You see life everywhere. You are inconsequential in the bigger scheme of things. You live in the world. The world does not exist or live for you. Your presence is what you make of it. How you react and how you think are in your control. So be at peace with your feelings and stay above the noise."

Before Candice could acknowledge or pursue the conversation further, the priest stood up and, dusting his clothing, pointed at the small crowd that seemed to have finished and was now ready to move.

Candice thanked him for his insights, her mind filled with new perspectives. The priest smiled, reminding her to embrace life in all its forms, for, in doing so, one finds their path to peace and understanding.

Departing from the hallowed grounds, Candice felt the eternal bond with Prince Bhanwar and Neelam etching deeply within her soul, a testament to their everlasting love transcending life and demise.

Encircled tightly together, everyone's pace was measured as they solemnly scooped up the ash remnants beneath them. A grave quietude saturated the atmosphere; everyone was trapped by their introspective sea of thoughts and feelings. The ache in Candice's heart mirrored the collective sorrow enveloping them all.

Standing around the twin brass urns that symbolised the departed lovers, a profound stillness overtook the gathering. Candice felt an inexplicable pull towards the gravity of the unfolding ceremony. The filling of the urns with ashes seemed to draw out intense heartache and unyielding fortitude from those present. They were part of something larger than life itself, a transformative rite of monumental significance.

The urns were filled, and the group started to break away gently, everyone quietly recognising the magnitude of the shared experience. The cleansing ritual that followed, where each washed away the soot from hands and feet, signified an act of purification and the commencement of a saga of healing. As Candice cast a long look at Andrew through misty eyes, she sensed an emerging strength and purpose burgeoning inside her, even amidst this new chapter fraught with unknowns.

A subtle changeover occurred as they journeyed towards the airport. The group's earlier heavy air gave way to lighter spirits, their conversations now soft yet brimming with thankful reflections and warm goodbyes. Walking through the lively terminal, they were touched by the gentle sun, its rays casting meaningful shadows upon their bittersweet transitions. While carrying burdensome hearts, they also had the unmistakable stirrings of anticipation for what lay ahead, uncertain yet filled with promise.

Candice's journey to Dehradun was a quiet interlude of anticipation and introspection. Staring through the plane window, her thoughts meandered like the terrain below. Once they landed, a team led by Vaibhav Bhati awaited their arrival.

While only an hour long, the drive to Haridwar felt timeless. Serpentine roads snaked around the mountains, presenting a charm that was both enchanting and tortuously slow. Ascending into the Himalayan foothills, the tapestry of nature unfurled before them with stunning grandeur. Emerald hills stretched endlessly, spattered with quaint hamlets and stair-like farms etched into the mountain flanks. Forest canopies clung to the inclines, exuding aromatic whiffs into the highland breeze. Distant summits sparkled under the solar caress.

For Candice, each curve in the journey unveiled new splendours—waterfalls that danced off precipices, weaving rainbows in their misty descent. Rivers frolicked on stone pathways, their cerulean ripples birthing airy rapids. Occasionally, ancient stone sanctuaries emerged, their orange pennants dancing atop stacked roofs. Cosy cottages with wooden frames and earthen exteriors huddled within leafy nooks.

Their driver offered empathetic smiles through the mirror, resonating with Candice's marvel at the profound allure of these lands – a reverie shared by pilgrims since time immemorial as they ventured to Haridwar, a cradle of Hindu sanctity. Welcoming the cool mountain zephyrs through her window, Candice felt a surge of energy.

Reaching the vibrant banks of the sacred Ganges, they were greeted by a priest. Amidst recitations of holy verses with Baba Kanmal, they delved into the river's frosty embrace. Clinging to a metallic lifeline bridging two pillars, Candice sensed a pull toward something transcendent. The river's symphony, accompanied by the amphitheatre of peaks, set a divine stage for their rites.

They knitted tighter bonds within their circle in this confluence of the earthly and the ethereal. As chants ascended, they entrusted flower petals to the currents, a tribute to the cherished Neelam's legacy.

At the peaceful culmination of their sacred observance, two intricately decorated vessels were carried with reverence to the brink of the Ganges. In a solemn procession, each participant had their moment beside the swirling waters to tenderly scatter Neelam's remnants. Candice's hand trembled as the ashes merged with the river, her heart heavy with unspoken sorrow.

She turned to Sandhya and Andrew, her voice a whisper, "Our mourning encompasses more than what's visible — an unseen life was also claimed in this sorrowful event. Only two urns mark Neelam and Bhanwar's passage, yet another soul departed with them." With a shared understanding, Sandhya and Andrew offered silent tributes; their visages bowed in homage.

Without realising it, Candice's fingers wrapped around the pendant holding snapshots of Jadene and Chris; they, too, occupied her thoughts.

Gazing beyond the ceremony, she locked eyes with Andrew, finding him seated alone further along the river, a solemn figure amid nature's flow. With his attention on the petals that danced upon the water, he sought comfort in this delicate goodbye to the departed spirits.

Drawing closer to Andrew, Candice discerned his silhouette quiver, a cascade of grief rolling down his cheeks. She paused, debating whether solitude was his ally at this moment, yet empathy prevailed.

As the distance between them closed, Andrew rose abruptly, poised to descend to the stream's precipice. Candice's concern drew her hand to his shoulder, steadying him against the river's embrace.

"Why are you going in there?" she asked, calming her voice.

Andrew looked at her sorrowfully, expressing his desire to return to this place since Pushpa had passed away. He wanted to honour her by immersing himself in the sacred waters. With determination in his eyes, he held onto a nearby chair for support and slowly lowered himself into the river.

Candice observed him, her heart heavy with empathy for the pain he must bear. Memories of her own departed—Jadene and Chris—swirled through her thoughts. Compelled by an unspoken solidarity, she walked beside him into the river. Icy currents enwrapped her suddenly, a bolt of cold jolting her balance on the slick riverbed, yet in a swift motion,

Andrew's steady hand prevented her fall. A warmth bloomed within Candice as their gazes locked, her cheeks colouring beneath his watchful eye.

"Still an atheist?" Andrew quipped with a sparkle of humour as they stepped out of the water.

Overcome with the flood of stirred emotions, Candice remained silent. A wave of peace and calmness enveloped them back onshore. The river seemed to have washed more than just the physical, imbuing them with a sense of rebirth. Sandhya was with them now, and their collective laughter at each other's dampened state filled the air, a testament to their bond.

Standing on the riverbank, they were greeted by a breathtaking light display. Countless enchanting lamps adorned the shore, glowing gently and radiantly upon everything around them. The air was filled with the symphony of chimes and celestial choral verses, creating a melody that seemed straight out of a myth or legend, surrounding the scene with an enchanting harmony. Candice felt a surge of awe and wonder, her eyes wide and sparkling as she took in the beauty of the sight. She felt a profound connection to something larger than herself, a sense of belonging and reverence she had never experienced.

At that moment, Candice felt transported back to a distant era, enveloped in an ancient and timeless ritual that had been performed for countless centuries. This experience left her not just humbled but deeply grateful as well. It was as if something far more significant than herself was at play here. The warm, humid air carried the rich scent of incense, filling their senses and providing comfort and reassurance.

Above them, the stars shimmered with unparalleled brilliance, each resembling a precious gem against the velvety night sky. The full moon bestowed its gentle, luminous glow upon them, casting an almost divine blessing upon the scene. Andrew wrapped his arm around her shoulders, drawing her closer to his side. He smiled at her tenderly, his eyes reflecting the light of the lamps and the moon. He kissed her softly on the forehead, making her heart skip a beat.

As they settled onto the soft, grassy riverbank, a sense of wonder escaped their lips as they sat silently, their eyes entirely captivated by the unfolding spectacle. Each melodic note of the prayers being sung seemed to infuse every lamp lining the riverbank with an even brighter sparkle as if imbued with the power of the enchanting song. The delicately crafted lamps floated gently on the water's surface, creating a mesmerising trail of light that stretched as far as the eye could see. The water lapping against the shore added a soothing rhythm to the music, creating a perfect harmony of nature and spirit. Utterly spellbound by the sheer beauty and magic of the moment, they felt as if they had been transported to a different time, a time of tradition and reverence.

When the prayer finally ended, it felt like hours had passed, though only a few minutes had slipped by in this otherworldly place. Basking in the peace and serenity surrounding them, Candice turned to Andrew with a soft expression. Her eyes glistened with unspoken emotions. She felt joy and sadness, knowing that this was one of the last moments they would share in this incredible journey. She wanted to make it last, to savour every second of it.

"I want to return to Jodhpur for another week before going back home to Johannesburg," she said, her voice barely above a whisper, her gaze locked with Andrew's. "Would you be my guide and show me around? But please, promise me no more adventures!"

Her heart fluttered with anticipation as Andrew slid his palm into hers, reassuringly squeezing it. At that moment, she knew these upcoming days could be the perfect culmination of their unforgettable journey together. He gently leaned in and kissed her softly, making her feel a wave of warmth and happiness. He nodded and whispered in her ear, "Anything for you, my dear."

Chapter 20:

Curse Unwound

"There is in every true woman's heart a spark of heavenly fire, which lies dormant in the broad daylight of prosperity, but which kindles up, beams, and blazes in the dark hour of adversity."

– The Sketch Book by Washington Irving

Resting her hands on her expansive balcony's intricately crafted wrought-iron railing, Candice savoured the bustling cityscape of Sandton, Johannesburg. It had been seven months since she had left Haridwar's tranquillity to return to her homeland's familiar surroundings. She was on the phone with Andrew, who was still in India. Meanwhile, Sandhya joined her on the balcony, carrying two glasses of freshly squeezed orange juice. As Sandhya tenderly placed her hands on Candice's growing baby bump, she excitedly chatted with her father on the phone, bringing a smile to Candice's face and making her feel at peace amidst life's transitions.

"Dad, isn't it amazing? Candice has grown so much, and I can already feel the baby kicking. I hope it's a brother who can bring balance to our family!"

Sandhya shared enthusiastically, eagerly anticipating the expansion of their family.

The doorbell interrupted their call. "They've arrived!" Sandhya exclaimed, a blend of surprise and delight illuminating her face.

Casually approaching the door, Candice opened it to find Vaibhav Bhati, her classmate from law school, and his ageing father, Avinash, who stood using a walking stick, his grey hair gently swaying in the breeze. Astonished by his remarkable recovery, Candice marvelled at the difference from the frail man she remembered.

"Mr. Bhati, I can hardly believe it's you. What an incredible transformation since our last meeting," Candice expressed, genuine amazement in her voice.

With a vibrant spirit, Avinash focused intently on Candice and warmly smiled, expressing his deep gratitude. "I owe my life to you," he stated with emotion. "I've come to show you the impact of your compassion on me."

Avinash's acknowledgement deeply moved Candice, knowing that her actions had profoundly changed his life.

As they drew closer, Candice observed a rejuvenated Avinash exuding grace. In a moment of insight, she declared, "This isn't just an end to misfortune; it's something immensely positive."

Avinash clasped her hand firmly, celebrating his liberation from longstanding hardships and his determination to embrace life fully. "The spiritual liberation I've experienced will always be with me. Whether mental resilience conquered my afflictions or not, my existence has been greatly expanded," he explained.

Candice lovingly touched her belly, feeling grateful for the blessing of motherhood. She tenderly caressed the locket bearing images of Jadene and Chris, whispering affectionately, "And my own life has been enriched through this experience."

Avinash took a deep breath and said, "Candice, I have an important mission. In recent weeks, I've been planning projects to aid underprivileged children in South Africa and India. My restored health highlighted how crucial your support was for me, motivating me to support those lacking educational and healthcare opportunities." He paused for emphasis before elaborating further. "We're establishing schools, orphanages, and medical clinics in remote villages to empower children out of poverty. Initially, we'll reach over 5,000 children, yet there's much more to do," Avinash disclosed his initial ambitions for the initiative.

Excitedly, Avinash implored, "Knowing your charitable spirit, I'm here to ask whether you'd lead our project as CEO?" He eagerly added, "Your help years ago inspired me to give back. With you on board, we can inspire hope across South Africa and India."

Candice contemplated Avinash's compelling invitation. Her resolve surged as she realised this was an opportunity to make substantial contributions beyond her imminent motherhood.

After careful consideration, she replied, "This aligns with my goals. Shall we wait for Sandhya's sibling, the newest family member, or begin our work immediately?"

Avinash smiled warmly at her. "The newest family member can join us along the way. Our work cannot wait any longer," he said determinedly.

With that, Candice joined hands with Avinash to embark on a journey that would not only change their lives but also impact thousands of children in need. Together, they were turning an ancestral curse into a generative opportunity, and Candice knew this was just the beginning of something great. She beamed radiantly.

--- The End ---